MAKING
A WHORE

Vũ Trọng Phụng
(1912-1939)

was a renowned Vietnamese writer and journalist, regarded as one of the most influential figures in twentieth century Vietnamese literature. In his short lifespan of 27 years, Vũ Trọng Phụng left an astonishing body of works across genres, from short story and novel to play and journalism. His writings are known for their bold and uncompromising portrayal of Vietnamese society under French colonial rule, and for addressing taboo topics such as sexuality and sex work. His works were banned in the north of Vietnam, then nationally until the late 1980s.

Đinh Ngọc Mai

is a non-binary writer of both academic and creative texts. They graduated from Mount Holyoke College with a Bachelor's in English Literature, and Hanoi National University of Education with a Master's in Literary Theory. Their research focuses on queer theory and queer Vietnamese and Asian American literature, tapping into the intellectual excitement and critical empathy that a queer Asian diaspora can enable and liberate.

Major Books

is an independent press dedicated to bringing
Vietnamese literature to the English-speaking world. Our
name speaks as a clear, bold, and audacious resistance
against the 'minor' status attributed to certain languages
and their literature in the global publishing scene. Ranging
from critically acclaimed post-war fiction, national epic
poetry, to contemporary LGBTQIA+ writings, we hope
to present a well-rounded portrait of Vietnam and our
diverse voices. Our hope is to contribute, no matter how
little, to growing awareness that there are no 'lesser'
voices in world literature.

Praises

'A classic work of Vietnamese literature. Heart-shattering, thought-provoking and unforgettable.'

—Nguyễn Phan Quế Mai, author of *Dust Child*

'*Making a Whore* is an immediate and sharply observed modernist text. While Vũ Trọng Phụng's prolific yet short-lived output of work was once considered obscene and outrageous, *Making a Whore* is an absolutely vital text that looks to the future by questioning the teachings of governance; the failings of the health, marriage and education systems, and how society shames young women and curious minds. Not only that, it is also a heartfelt treatise on a person's capacity for love and desire, and the systems in place that restrict them.'

—Joshua Jones, author of *Local Fires*

Major Books Ltd, 128 City Road, London, United Kingdom, EC1V 2NX

First published in the United Kingdom in 2024 by Major Books

Làm Đĩ was written by Vũ Trọng Phụng in 1936
The original work belongs to the public domain

Originally published in Vietnamese as Làm Đĩ in 1937 by Mai Lĩnh publishing house

Translation copyright © 2024 Đinh Ngọc Mai

Cover Art © 2024 Nguyễn Thanh Vũ

Edited by Alina Martin, Dương Mạnh Hùng, and Samuel Tan

A CIP catalogue record for this book is available from the British Library

ISBN 978-1-917233-00-2

eISBN 978-1-917233-01-9

Typeset in Garamond Premier Pro by Coral Books JSC

Printed and bound in Vietnam by Hai Phong Stationery Joint Stock Company

www.major-books.com

Vũ Trọng Phụng

MAKING A WHORE

Translated by Đinh Ngọc Mai

MAJOR BOOKS

Table of content:

Introduction

Making a Whore (*Làm Đĩ*) was written in late 1936 and early 1937 by the celebrated journalist and novelist, Vũ Trọng Phụng, widely considered twentieth century Vietnam's greatest writer. During a brief career, cut short in 1939 by his tragic death from tuberculosis at the age of 27, Vũ Trọng Phụng produced a massive and distinguished body of writing. It includes seven complete novels, five book-length works of non-fiction reportage, several dozen short stories, a handful of plays, and hundreds of columns of professional journalism.[1] Without exception, all of Vũ Trọng Phụng's writing, even the fiction, appeared in print initially in the pages of the same Vietnamese language press that employed him. Vũ Trọng Phụng's rootedness in the commercial press helps to explain the 'newsy' preoccupations of his writing: local politics, global affairs, the growth of the market economy, the rise of inequality and class conflict, the spread of crime, and changes in Vietnamese gender relations, and sexual culture under French colonial rule.

Vũ Trọng Phụng's background as a newspaperman was instrumental as well in the first great commercial successes upon which his celebrity was built—a series

---

[1] For a full accounting, see Peter Zinoman, *Vietnamese Colonial Republican: The Political Vision of Vũ Trọng Phụng* (Berkeley: University of California Press, 2014)

of works of long-format investigative reportage about the seamy underside of life in Hà Nội, the colonial capitol city. In 1933, he published *The Man Trap* (*Cạm Bẫy Người*), a profile of small-time con men who staged rigged games of chance on the sidewalks of Hà Nội's old quarter. The following year, he released *The Industry of Marrying Westerners* (*Kỹ Nghệ Lấy Tây*) a wickedly funny profile of interracial conjugal relations in the colony. His later works in the genre explored the lives of household servants and actors, and the internal workings of Hà Nội's largest venereal disease clinic.[1] Given Vũ Trọng Phụng's penchant for timely and sensational topics, it is no surprise that entrepreneurial publishers competed fiercely to secure the lucrative rights to republish his best-selling work.

Together with *The Storm* (*Giông Tố*), *Dumb Luck* (*Số Đỏ*), and *The Dike Breaks* (*Vỡ Đê*), *Making a Whore* is one of four novels that Vũ Trọng Phụng wrote and released in serial form as part of an unprecedented surge of literary productivity, stretching from January 1936 to March, 1937.[2] During the four peak months (October 1936 to January 1937) of this astonishing fifteen-month span, serialized chapters of three of the novels—*Dumb Luck*, *The Dike Breaks* and *Making a Whore*—could be read

---

[1] *Cơm Thầy Cơm Cô* ('Household servants'), 1935, *Vẽ Nhọ Bôi Hề* ('Clown makeup'), 1934 and *Lục Xì* ('VD clinic'), 1938.

[2] *The Storm* started on January 2, 1936 in *Hà Nội Newspaper* ('Hà Nội Báo') and concluded seven months later on September 30, 1936. *Dumb Luck* began in the same paper one week later and ran for three months from October 7, 1936 to January 20, 1937. *Making a Whore* first appeared on August 8, 1936 and ended on March 27, 1937. And on September 27, 1936, *Tuesday Novel* ('Tiểu Thuyết Thứ Ba') began serializing *The Dike Breaks* which, given its length, must have run into the early months of 1937.

simultaneously in three different weekly newspapers, two in Hà Nội and one in Huế. It is tempting to assume that Vũ Trọng Phụng produced this massive quantity of prose at the expense of literary quality, but nothing could be further from the truth. Vietnamese readers today recognise the historical significance and literary value of all four works, with *The Storm* and *Dumb Luck* widely viewed as two of twentieth century Vietnam's best novels.

The extraordinary quantity and quality of Vũ Trọng Phụng's novelistic quartet during 1936-37 is matched by its remarkable diversity. *The Storm* is a sprawling family melodrama set against the backdrop of political intrigue and class struggle across a deeply fragmented rural-urban divide. *Dumb Luck* is an absurdist farce that skewers the pretentions and status anxieties of Hà Nội's nouveau riche. And *The Dike Breaks* embodies a localized socialist realism in its concern with the 'enlightenment through struggle' of a Vietnamese political activist.

Freud and *Making a Whore*

Published between August 8, 1936 and March 27, 1937 in Huế's *Perfume River* (*Sông Hương*), *Making a Whore*, departs from the other three novels in tone, structure, and content. Adopting a radically experimental approach and focused forthrightly on local sexual culture, *Making a Whore* is the first Vietnamese novel shaped explicitly by the Freudian theories that penetrated the colony in the early 1930s.[1] In an introduction to the novel, Vũ Trọng Phụng mentioned Freud by name (along with Goethe, Schiller, Yên Đổ and Nguyễn Công Trứ) as one of several thinkers who inspired him to take sexual matters seriously. Reviewers of the novel also highlighted its debt to Freud. 'With the book *Making a Whore*, Vũ Trọng Phụng has pushed his pen in the direction of science, knocking on the door of Sigmund Freud and asking to join his school,' wrote Minh Tước in the short-lived journal *New* (*Mới*) on May 15, 1939. 'He is clearly developing an understanding of psychoanalysis from the Austrian professor. *Making a Whore* reads like it was crafted from Freud's lectures.'[2]

Many aspects of *Making a Whore* bear the imprint of Freud including its central focus on the link between the descent of its main character, Huyền, into a life of prostitution, and the repression of her normal sexual drives during childhood and puberty. To explain why an intelligent girl from an elite family, falls into commercial sex work, the novel divides her life into sequential periods that resemble the 'stages' of psychosexual development in Freudian theory. Zeroing in on the significance of puberty, the novel centers Huyền's subjection to forms of repression and misinformation during these years that distorted her sexual development and damaged her mental health. The end of the novel reveals that its content has been drawn

---

[1] Peter Zinoman, *Vietnamese Colonial Republican: The Political Vision of Vũ Trọng Phụng*: 139-140.

[2] Minh Tước, 'Đọc Sách Làm Đĩ', in *Mới*, May 15, 1939. p.8.

from a confessional notebook read aloud to the narrator by Huyền, a source that conjures the 'talking treatments' characteristic of Freudian analysis.

Pornography, Science, and Sex Education

While a few critics dwelled on the Freudian content of *Making a Whore*, most discourse about the novel joined a bitter debate over whether it should be denounced as pornography or praised as a bold contribution to science and sex education.[1] Vũ Trọng Phụng's antagonists in the debate were a mix of Catholic priests, self-styled Confucian intellectuals, and writers associated with the aggressively modernizing Self-Reliance Literary Group (Tự Lực Văn Đoàn). Members of this odd conservative alliance denounced Making a Whore for stoking sexual desire for monetary gain. Vũ Trọng Phụng's most vocal supporter was Phan Khôi, the editor of *Perfume River* and one of the most brilliant and influential Vietnamese intellectuals of the colonial era. Rejecting the charge that the explicit treatment of sexuality in the novel was pornographic, Phan Khôi praised Vũ Trọng Phụng as a reformer who believed that surfacing social pathologies in the most forthright terms was the only way to effectively combat them. 'To be blunt, we need to talk about sexual intercourse,' Phan Khôi began.

---

[1] On August 9, Phan Khôi, received a letter from the Catholic priest J.M. Thích threatening to boycott the paper and denouncing the novel as a work of pornography. See, Phan Khôi, 'Thơ Trả Lời Một Ông Cố Đạo', *Sông Hương*, (August 22, 1936): 4.

Sexual intercourse is crucial for human beings, but it is also a dangerous thing. It is not dangerous in and of itself but because people have done bad things because of it. Masturbation, extramarital sex, nymphomania, prostitution. The spread of disease, crime, the weakening of the race, the corruption of society: all because of sexual intercourse. Obviously, this is an urgent problem on par with other national problems in politics, economics and education.

Opinion on the topic is divided into two camps. The first camp possesses a poor attitude. They know that this corrosive problem needs to be solved but they think it should be solved in silence and only after it has spread. They don't dare to teach what should be taught about sexual intercourse <u>before</u> people commit mistakes or catch sexually transmitted diseases. They fear that bringing up the topic might inadvertently gin up curiosity about it. Members of this camp include politicians, religion officials, and Confucian scholars.

The rival camp includes scientists, especially physicians. They examine the root of the problem which is ignorance. For them, it is worse to punish someone after they commit a crime or treat someone with medicine after they get sick. They know it's better to address ignorance, so they won't commit a crime or get sick in the first place. This camp's attitude is bold and positive; it openly addresses topics that some prefer to hide.

Between these two camps, *Perfume River* favors the second one.... To express our support for this camp, we promote its mission in our newspaper by publishing *Making a Whore*.[1]

In an interview with the critic Lê Thanh, published in *Bắc Hà Magazine* the following year, Vũ Trọng Phụng confirmed Phan Khôi's description of the pedagogic mission behind the novel. It is critical, he argued, 'to acknowledge the natural sexual desires of pubescent girls who lack sufficient education—an issue I address in *Making a Whore*. I wrote that novel after reading the translation of a German book that compiles the darkest confessions of young students. After reading this brave, scientific book, I understood that puberty must be driving our youth toward masturbation and perversity, and I began to see the urgent necessity of sex education. If only people can study the terms and topics that have long been considered filthy, perhaps there will be less real filth in the future.'[2]

Making a Whore's diagnosis of the sexual crisis afflicting Vietnamese society goes beyond the deleterious effects of repression (in a Freudian sense) and insufficient education. Other major culprits in the novel are 'materialism' (in contrast to spiritualism) and 'individualism.' In the

---

[1] Phan Khôi, 'Một Vấn Đề, Hai Ý Kiến', *Sông Hương*, no. 11 (October 10, 1936)
[2] Lê Thanh, 'Chúng Tôi Phỏng Vấn Ông Vũ Trọng Phụng Về Những Tiểu Thuyết "Giông Tố," "Làm Đĩ."' [I interview Mr. Vũ Trọng Phụng about his novels *The Storm* and *Making a Whore*], Bắc Hà, Hà Nội, no.2 (April 8, 1937).

end, capitalism plays a role in Huyền's demise as well, since she runs out of money and must ultimately sell her body to survive. In *Making a Whore*, the fusion of these mismatched traditional and modern elements—Confucian prudishness, patriarchy, materialism, individualism, and capitalism—is seen to have yielded a toxic Vietnamese sexual culture that the novel has been written to combat.

Although *Making a Whore* is not considered one of Vũ Trọng Phụng's great novels, it provides a dramatic example of his enduring preoccupation with the complex relationship between sex, gender, and capitalism—a preoccupation threaded through many of his most important works. It also shines a bright light onto aspects of cultural and intellectual life in late colonial Vietnam that are rarely given sufficient attention. The centering of the sexual crisis of Vietnamese society in *Making a Whore* during a period known mainly for political struggles between colonialism, nationalism and communism expands our understanding of the range of concerns that animated civic-minded Vietnamese during this tumultuous era.

Peter Zinoman, UC Berkeley

In Lieu of a Preface

Making a Whore is a realistic novel whose purpose is to urge moralists and parents to care for their children's happiness and to pay attention to what corrupt prejudices still consider dirty: that is, sexuality.

The author chooses not to follow those who use flowery language and call it 'love', nor those who timidly refer to it as 'copulation'. Instead, the author uses its frank, colloquial name because they firmly believe that this matter is more closely tied to the flesh than to the soul. While it can be divided into two aspects, it is more physiologically accurate to consider it as one. The physical and spiritual elements harmonise with each other, and only when the body's desires are satisfied can spiritual love truly flourish. To speak of ideal love without acknowledging lust is merely the practice of unrealistic dreamers.

A novel that exists to serve sex?

Moralists, please refrain from condemnation! Sex is not evil; rather, it is a noble, beautiful, and profoundly sacred thing. Thanks to it, humanity persists, and we exist. The author invites you to consider the perspectives of Freud, Goethe, Schiller, Yên Đổ, and Nguyễn Công Trứ on whether sex is truly dirty and unworthy of mention. Surely that should suffice. So then, esteemed readers—you who claim to be virtuous yet are just like me, like my brothers! Why is it that this very thing, which people outwardly consider proper and moral to never mention aloud, is the same thing that may occupy their private thoughts at any moment?

Sex belongs to the realm of physiology, not morality; it cannot be controlled by ethical principles...

Sex is as necessary for the mortal flesh as food. Therefore, 'noble love' is merely a form of love in which physical desires remain unfulfilled—in other words, it is simply frustrated love. When love is frustrated, people elevate it by calling it 'noble love, pure love, ideal love, or spiritual love'.

In civilised countries, people do not shy away from discussing sexuality. On the contrary, they study and analyse it to educate each other about sexual matters. Extensive research, experience, and scholarly education have thoroughly examined the issue of sexuality, elevating it to a level of understanding that benefits society. Books, articles, and public forums have saved countless young men and women from debauchery. Yet, the importance of sex education is so great that no amount of ink or paper seems sufficient to address it fully.

A professor at the University of Berlin, Mr. W. Liepman, stated:

'Youth and love—this issue can be called the great

tragedy of love. Due to current ignorance and misguided education, humanity's noblest pleasure undergoes numerous tribulations before it can be enjoyed, if it isn't prematurely ruined and cast into the gutter.'

It's time for us to pay attention to this matter today.

The meeting of East and West on this strip of land has strongly influenced our material lives. What could be more absurd than having accepted the new lifestyle, which includes theatres, cinemas, modern clothes, dancing houses, perfumes, and waxes, which are conditions that make humanity more and more SEXUAL, but at the same time not recognising the need to propagate the issue of education about SEXUALITY, in order to teach future generations how *to sex* ethically, *to sex* honestly, and *to sex* in a way that will not cause harm to your race?

This Vietnamese society has truly begun to plunge into sexual chaos!

The enormous enrichment of venereal healers, the prosperity of dance parlours, the increase in the number of gangsters, abortions, and crimes of passion reported daily in the newspapers are evidence enough. In particular, the world-weariness leading to suicide among some teenagers, along with incidents of rape, further support this observation.

Faced with such a situation, what good is it to anyone to merely fold one's arms and lament, 'Oh, the decadence!'

Finding an ethical framework for sexuality and educating teenagers clearly about sex are tasks that must be undertaken immediately...

Young men and women in puberty, when their bodies are aflame with the excitement of silent changes and development of sexual organs, are very susceptible to mistakes and easily harmed if parents do not teach them what they need to know and shield them from negative influences...

Why do people consider sex unimportant or dirty? Why are people so wilfully ignorant and hypocritical? Why don't we dare to talk about the things that preoccupy all types of people? Why don't we dare to discard unreasonable shame and teach about sexual organs, which god has dared to give to humanity without shame?

Whether to speak or be silent, to educate each other about regulating lust to beautify life, or to just let human lust cause chaos in humanity—that's the crux of why a society will prosper or decline.

For these reasons, *Making a Whore* was born.

It will make the 'traditional' moralists wince.

It will make people who don't want to understand anything cry, 'Oh, the decadence!'

But the author still has hope in those who think...

Vũ Trọng Phụng

When parents lack in the disposition to pass down this noble heritage to their children, in an entirely ethical manner and with a full understanding of the biological principles relevant to the child's age and level of intelligence, then an utterly reprehensible confusion will persistently defile the very gift that nature has endowed us with. This failure will obstruct our future generations, leaving them with no guidance on the path to ultimate goodness and beauty.

Professor W. Liepmann, L'Éducation Sexuelle

In the Beginning

On the wall, the clock measuredly chimed seven.

With the dining table cleared, Quý sat in front of a cup of hot water, a toothpick slack from his mouth, wrinkles scrunched up on his forehead. A dazed look of contemplation on his face while his arms hung loose with exhaustion and lethargy... He lay on the chair at an angle, legs stretched, head leaning slightly forward, arms drooping low as if falling off onto the ground— a truly depressing sight.

I said,

'Sit up straight, will you? You look like one mortally wounded man withering away on a stretcher, or a hitman's victim, even!'

'What bull!'

He responded nonchalantly and remained seated all the same.

Down in the kitchen, my wife was still preoccupied with cleaning up. Sneaking a few glances back and forth, I gestured to him.

'Let's head out?'

Still mopey, he said,

'Sure, if you say so. But... where?'

I whispered,

'Some booze, bawdiness, bong, and... betting.'

He laughed half-heartedly, doubtful,

'Not a chance! Surely you know that I... at least for now, I'm an esteemed educator!'

'You know what I hate the most? Posers!'

He lifted his chin up to taunt me instead of answering.

The two of us sat in silence for a long while.

Quý and I had always been the closest of friends. Our bond dated back to our days of shaved heads, when we attended preparatory school together. Our friendship was illuminated by the numerous times when he sacrificed himself for me and put up with me, when we played đánh đáo[1] in the school yard, scavenging for marbles in all sorts of sewers, hunted for crickets on Sundays, chased after cicadas on summer nights, and hung out around tree trunks... There were times when we fought, or when we sat in class with dazed faces as if we were listening intently to the teacher, but in fact we were tapering the bottoms of our pen holders to stab each other's thighs to death... Sometimes, when he found a colossal cicada that he wouldn't let me play with, I'd plan my revenge. After the class quieted down and the teacher grabbed the chalk and ruler, I'd gently slide my hand into his bag and squeeze the cicada until its 'eek eek' shriek tore through the room. Three slaps from the teacher—and Quý would end up kneeling on the veranda. Hate, love, love, hate: we had unknowingly practised a sophisticated and astute philosophy normally taught to boys and girls—that is, if they wanted to sustain their love and prevent their domestic lives from dulling like the surface of a stagnant pond. Sticking pieces of paper saying, 'I'm a thief' on each other's back, breaking each other's pen tips during đích-tê lessons for no reason, sneaking an ink bottle right underneath the crotch when one was standing up to read texts out loud—to express our affection, our mischief knew no bounds. After silent wars where we branded each other as archenemies, some nonsensical and trivial

---

1 A Vietnamese traditional game revolving around chucking coins.

event was enough to restore our friendship. Cats and dogs, he and I. All in all, we were a duo of classmates who deserved to be role models for this generation and the one after, too.

When we reached middle school, we started to drift apart. I stayed in school for a few more years before quitting and wading into a career in writing. Quý persisted in a teacher's school for what seemed like forever, then ended up dinning letters into children after he graduated.

Since then, people bestowed on him the divine duty of lecturing yokels in the depths of jungles and caves that hadn't the slightest clue what civilisation was, teaching them that *café* is 'coffee shop'; *le café* is 'brewed coffee'. *Mère* is 'mother'; *la mère* is 'the mother'. We were truly on our separate ways then. Once in a while, there'd be a letter going in, a letter going out, but all the news was as dry as dust, since there was nothing but the mundane and trivial—yet essential—exchanges about the welfare of each other's household.

To be fair, when we first drifted apart, something often felt amiss... Quý and I quickly faded from each other's life, wrapped in the struggle to make ends meet, but perhaps like me, he, too, often reminisced about our childhood years, ablaze with zest, innocent nuisance, and harmless mischief: I'd write him verses to woo the ladies, and he'd foot the bill for my movie tickets.

Not long afterward, I heard word that his father had him marry the daughter of a lavishly wealthy chief. She was a village girl, chunky as a chum and sooty as a chimney. Even when he spared her no glance, she was smitten with him, jealous all the time, and even worse, riddled with bad habits. So in short, his entire life was railroaded into misery! For two whole years, I'd chuckle at the thought of Quý, delighting in his depressing love life as karmic retribution. I no longer had to exact vengeance on him for that time long ago when we were dreaming up our future and the ins and outs of fishing for a pretty wife. He had always spurned my earthbound aspirations as painfully pedestrian.

Two years later, he sent me a letter. Roped into fatherhood, he complained that he already had two daughters who, alas, looked exactly like their mother! Then the endless trivialities about his wife's pregnancy, his children's maladies, his preoccupation with others' joys and woes, death anniversaries, lunar holidays, farewell rituals, arrears... Such were the utter banalities that bound humans to an invisible string of attachment. Our mutual dependence led to mutual misery, suffocating our spirit, passion, and optimism.

One day at noon, I came across Quý the teacher

dressed in a yellow Western suit and pull-up leather shoes, looking as dazed as if he had lost all will to live. He was sauntering companionless in the heart of Hà Nội, yet he had the expression of someone who strayed into an alien society. Ecstatic, I bolted up to grab him. I tagged along with him to buy a spirit lamp and invited him home for dinner. To elaborate on our elation at this much-awaited reunion between brothers-in-arms would be superfluous.

As we were getting plastered, Quý boasted about his promotion as an eighth-grade teacher, while his wife became increasingly irksome by the day, his daughters grew up to become their mother by the day, his cat had delivered two litters of three calico cats, and so on...

As he could stay for only a day or two, I wanted to take him out to lift his spirits and treat him with the utmost decorum, so that he could witness how civilised and advanced our grand city had become. And, to be honest, for the past few months, I'd felt like I'd been confined in a prison without a chance to break free and blow off steam. Now that my teacher friend from the great mountains was visiting for the summer, only a fool would miss out on the opportunity.

At once, I jumped to my feet and directed him.

'We're off!'

He stood up as I put on my jacket and went down to the kitchen. Against my plan to talk with my wife in private, my foolish friend suddenly decided to join. Before I could say anything, he had already begun, and ludicrously so.

'May I head out to pass some time with your husband?'

My wife feigned a friendly smile.

'Oh, who am I to say no? I hope you can come back around ten to be able to rest properly.'

Quý acquiesced in an instant. Enraged, I protested.

'Do you know how many old friends he has to meet? Ten is out of the question.'

'Cut the lies! Friends, my foot. He just said you'd head out to pass time. You see, my man here will find ways to rope you into some sleazy business, the lout that he is! He has none of your decency, so take heed!'

While my friend turned into a blockheaded yes-man, anger swelled bitterly in my throat. Do not mistake me for being the wife-fearing type; I was just being respectful. How could women, with their myopic minds and paltry hearts, fathom any cordial banter? Yes, although us men did mess around, no one would be so cold-blooded as to betray his own wife.

Taking my silence as fear—though it was actually out

of disdain—my wife continued,

'Enjoy yourself and please come back early to rest. You travelled a lot today...'

We left the house.

At first, I told Quý that in light of his visit, I'd gather some brothers for a booze-up in the suburbs... But who would've thought he'd vehemently refuse, more terrified of my wife than I!

'I haven't been back for ages. It'd be a downer if I gave your wife a reason to hold a grudge against me.' So he said!

From movie screenings and singing shows at dance clubs to whiling away the hours along the streets, we found nothing to our taste and eventually sought the joy of carnal delight. Now was my chance to show this Mán Xá[1] brother how far the sex trade had come. Quý also said his life in the jungle had kept him out of the loop, which was all the better.

A friend of mine, well-versed in all vices, clued me in on an Elysium inside a house on S.T. Street. A hefty sum of silver would guarantee me royal treatment and

---

[1] Mán Xá is the nickname that Vũ Trọng Phụng and his friends used to call the writer Lan Khai, who lived in Tuyên Quang and often wrote novels about people in the mountains and jungles.

intimacy from gorgeous women whom society exalted as elite. The madame, daughter of a mandarin chief, was as tactical as she was tight-lipped. Her punters could rest assured on all counts.

Having made up our minds, we called for a rickshaw.

Upon arriving at that street, the driver parked the rickshaw on the pavement, in front of a Western building whose exterior gave off the impression that the owner was a noble-minded citizen. Five minutes later, he turned around and told us to head in.

A few stairs up, Quý briskly placed his hand on my shoulder as if to hold me back, even when I had yet set a foot inside. I also felt on edge and stayed put; my stomach was churning at the thought of the driver having got the wrong address or the house itself having changed owners.

That's it! Even if you'd known debauchery inside out, had life down pat, and mastered all the veiled vices of society, you'd still find yourself fretting in this situation. You couldn't be so sure of yourself that you'd bet on a house such as this one being the base of a prostitution business. Mother-of-pearl cupboards, a mahogany plank bed from a Chinese lounge ensemble, an antique bureau as big as a bed, a molten brass burner set as huge as the one that Hạng Vũ lifted to flex his muscles, Jiangxi porcelain pots and pieces... With such wealth of possessions, if the owner wasn't a retired and revered mandarin, then they were surely a tycoon of some sort. The vacant and silent ambiance only magnified the solemnity of it all...

We were itching to retreat...

Suddenly, a young man rushed out to greet us, his feet bare but his clothes pristine. He bowed earnestly and ushered us in.

'Oh dear! Please come in, good sirs!'

And so we eased our minds, finding reassurance in his slanted smile. If he wasn't a valet or ma-cô, then his conduct would have never been so chummy to the point of cheeky, so chipper to the point of cocking a snook at the clients.

We went into the Chinese-style lounge, waiting for him to sit us down, but he went on,

'Oh dear, please come all the way in, good sirs...'

Through a narrow trail connected to the luxurious, outermost lounge, we crossed a courtyard, and then made our way through another tight trail sandwiched between unending walls. There was the occasional large door and window, left ajar or concealed with curtains or folding screens. Silence reigned within those rooms. Deep down, I was overjoyed to have visited on a day of slow business.

Passing another courtyard into a chamber with a Western sofa set, the young man finally invited us to sit. Outside the room, white shadows began to flit back and forth, gearing up to scout the right flowers for eagerly awaiting butterflies. After some time, the flapping sounds of coconut slippers against brick staircases signalled the madame's descent from upstairs.

'Good day, esteemed sirs.'

'The pleasure is all ours. Good day to you, madame.'

The madame lingered by the entrance, fastening the remaining button on her light blue tunic. Before restraining herself into modesty, her semi-revealing áo dài unveiled the row of lace on her corset, a massive pot-belly, and a pair of stocky thighs flickering behind paper-thin layers of batiste. Her appearance spoke volumes about her. Especially with her hair sloppily wrapped, she still exuded a coquettish allure despite her yellowing youth. Her seductive eyes, plump cheeks, scarlet lips... As I thought of men like us, the top brass, the machos, who had embraced her only to lose our fortune to her, my blood ran cold. What a terrifying woman she was. She had the power of a Western Madame, an elite ruler of prostitutes as depicted in the report *Les servantes du Démon*, the type of madame frequented by bank owners, section chiefs, ambassadors from other nations, who fixed up an official by securing for him the wife of another official, for this other official had stolen the vice minister position from him!

With grandeur she planted herself on the seat opposite us, lifted her hand to cover an exhausted yawn as if annoyed, then tossed out a question.

'Pardon me, good sirs, if I may be so rude as to inquire: are you local or from out of town?'

I glanced at my friend, signalling that his yellowed clothes had exposed him as a jungle man, and thus, humiliated me. Then I responded,

'Only my friend here is from out of town. I'm a local.'

She asked again.

'Have you ever been here?'

'A few months ago...'

'So the young sister must've served you that day?'

'Yes.'

'Then what do you fancy, brothers?'

How commendable was the flair of these madames; every new face would become familiar in an instant. Breaking out of his shell, Quý took the plunge and hastily asserted.

'Dear sister, we are fancying some... *amour*.'

She glanced left and right, then grinned.

'That's a given, but what else?'

My friend shot me a look, asking me to answer in his place. I said.

'Listen, sister, I just want to express my utmost care for my friend here, so do whatever you see fit... And what else do you have, anyway? Your best girl is probably Phù Dung, and maybe Lưu Linh[1] at the most, so why don't we invite them both for more festivity?'

'Wonderful!'

She cheered. Then her face became stern as she whispered,

'Behave yourself, okay brothers? What type of woman do you want? One or two? Us or the Chinese—or mixed?'

'Something domestic would be lovely.'

'Sure, and what kind? Modern or country? Or half-and-half?'

I handed over the selection to my friend with a glance.

---

[1] Phù Dung was the name for the goddess of opium; Lưu Linh, during the Tân Dynasty (4th-century China) was one of the seven scholars who lived in reclusion in a bamboo forest called 'Seven Sages of the Bamboo Grove,' who did nothing but drink.

He said.

'A modern peeress!'

The madame laughed.

'Those ladies are off the table. Who would hand them over so easily! Or perhaps...'

'A woman will do, any woman!'

'We must cover all bases now, because once I call on a woman, she must be usable. Exchanges and round trips are tedious for her and also bothersome for us. So however you want your product, lay it all out.'

'Then what do you have in stock, sister?'

'This place of courtship has people from all walks of life, while I, a Madame Moon, can weave hundreds of thousands of red strings of fate in all sizes and lengths[1]... How about the wives of officials and clerks who gambled their way into poverty?'

'Well-bred ladies only!' My friend twisted his lips.

'And are they not? Are well-bred ladies not allowed to be corrupt?'

'Wives of officials and clerks, or well-bred ladies, are

---

[1] Refers to an East Asian myth in which a lunar matchmaking god would bind invisible red strings on people's fingers to link them to their soulmates.

surely better than taxi-girls...'

The madame raised a hand, brushing off my friend's words...

'You must not know... The mistresses of officials and secretaries, though reputable in name, are mostly old hags as stiff as a stick. Don't underestimate taxi-girls. They're the ones in the know. They have countless ways to play coy and butter you up, that crafty bunch!'

'Sure, that works too.'

'So one or two?'

'Up to you.'

She gave it some thought and concluded.

'Two wouldn't be wasteful, yet one would hardly be miserly, either. If it's two, you have to use two chambers, as the women will only use the back door. This is a private space, not some licensed public parlour... Putting two women in one room will be quite the challenge.'

While we thought about how much this would set us back, she continued.

'Please do excuse me, my good sirs, and let's not beat around the bush... How much do you intend to spend on tonight's frolics?'

I said.

'No, it has to be taxi-girls. One chamber, one box of opium, two bottles of champagne, and one woman!'

Pulling out my wallet to get the silver, I added.

'Here, whatever is worthy of this money. I'll be back sooner or later anyway.'

'You don't have to tell me twice!'

She stepped out to the yard, screaming.

'Duyên! Take these two gentlemen to chamber four!'

Then she turned to us.

'While we're getting things ready, Duyên will keep the pipe warm for you both.'

She exited, followed by a yellow-toothed guy dressed in silk clothing. A petite lady came out to greet us and led us upstairs.

The room we entered was tastefully arranged, on par with luxurious Western hotel rooms, even. A mahogany plank attached to an opium tray set, a Hong Kong-style bed, and a sofa. In one corner, an adjustable body mirror. In another, a sink stacked with fresh, white cotton towels. On the wall, numerous photos of naked Western stunners clipped from pornographic magazines such as

Paris Plaisirs, *Eros*, and *Sex Appeal*.

The two of us took off our jackets and rested on the plank. Duyên sat hunched up, fixing the opium tray. First things first: I took a good look at Duyên's face and body. While she was indistinguishable from the hundreds of thousands of young ladies across brothels, her face bore an unusually striking innocence! Despite her profession, such innocence would surely cast doubt in your heart as you failed to find an alternative word to depict the purity of the weaker sex.

From then on, my friend laid solemnly on the plank, his spirit that of a remorseful husband who betrayed his wife by accident. Duyên lay down, dutifully cooking us opium. We started chatting away.

'Little sister! How old are you?'

'Although I'm like this, I'm already twenty-one. I look very young, don't I?'

'Are you the madame's daughter?'

'Yes, but adopted.'

'Do you have to serve often, then?'

'Only sometimes, because I already have a lover.'

'That's impressive! Who is he?'

'An old Western lawyer. He's head over heels for me!'

'Why aren't you married?'

'His old lady would throw a jealous fit. He can only manage to drop by this place; he wouldn't dare rent a house for me.'

'Then what kind of crowd usually comes here?'

'Oh, every kind! Foreign chiefs, soldiers, lawyers, judges, Indian loan sharks, restaurant tycoons, casino moguls, politicians, bigwigs, we got all of them...'

'The madame's business must be booming.'

'That's without a doubt.'

'Why is today so slow?'

'Wait until twelve and you'll see! In this house, day is night and night is day.'

'Little one, why are you so young yet already sullied?'

Hearing Quý's rather rude joke, Duyên twisted her lips and seized the chance to drag all men over the coals.

'I didn't want to say this, but what a bunch of selfish knaves you men are! The prostitution business was all your doing, and yet the women warped into this trade have to bear the brunt of your wigging and rollicking...

If not for your stone-hearted kind, us women wouldn't have been so screwed over. We'd just be at home with our parents, then a slick and dapper guy would pop out of thin air to woo us... He'd lead us by the nose into moral decay, only for cruel men to swarm into shame and taunt us even more! No one bats an eye at how loose you are, and yet when we let go even just a tiny bit, our whole lives are ruined! Oh heavens, you cads! You're utterly rotten!'

Even though Duyên went on that tangent in jest, I could sense the spite in her voice—and the logic behind it, too.

I blurted out,

'Have you felt troubled? Or regretful that your life turned out this way?'

Duyên, incredulous, asked back.

'Why? What's there to be troubled or regretful about?'

'That you couldn't marry a decent husband like everyone else and have to live a life you don't want...'

Duyên cackled.

'You ask the wackiest things. I have neither regret nor trouble. This life is... filthy, I know that much, but you get so used to it, it's practically a nonissue! Whatever job you have, as long as you get used to it, everything goes. Just look at those brothels on Hàng Mành Alley... As soon as they spot a squaddie, their gabby mouths fire out, "Hey, come have a taste if you're game!" How could there be such wasters among us, and you might be wondering: have they no shame? They must've been decent people before they got to this point! They must've had a roof over their head until seventeen or eighteen, before they could even go wild, right? Goodness, I couldn't wrap my head around it no matter how hard I tried... And then I realised that I just need to find my feet, then all is hunky-dory! Your mind might boggle for now, but if you just put yourself in my shoes, it's not that big of a deal. And you're missing the mark with your pity that I can't get married like everyone else. Why can't I? In old-school teachings, to whore is to dig your own grave. But does life actually work like that? In life, I see oodles of classy, honourable, and respectable women who mostly end up as spinsters, or married to wankers who sleep around, neglect them, and beat them. Meanwhile, the corrupt ones who whore themselves out can climb the ranks and marry loaded and lapdog husbands like child's play! Personally, I think all parents should take this to heart: if they want a prized son-in-law in this day and age, a corrupt daughter is a must-have.'

The two of us were left aghast, for the girl spoke nothing but the truth.

My friend suddenly decided to wax philosophical, lamenting Duyên's life story in French to shut her out. One wet blanket led to another, and our spirits soon soured! From blasting the rise of materialist tendencies sweeping through our civilisation to cussing out those menaces to humanity, we turned into cynics. While my friend's cynicism was probably genuine, I found it simply hilarious that any two-faced chap who played around would end up a grouchy smart-ass just like this. Pointing at Duyên, Quý spoke to me, still in French.

'Just see for yourself... Such a fair maiden, yet how wounded her soul, how woeful her plight! How come the Creator let such a marvel of nature fall from grace without batting an eye? How did society let someone go off the rails without a shred of regret?'

I held my friend back with a laugh.

'Watch your mouth! You know who also waffles like this? Men who chuck their wives for whores or get spliced with whores.'

Quý rushed to counter me.

'No! You're wrong! I'm not so compassionate that I'd bring whores home. Take a closer look at that girl's face, then think on it for a bit. W-What if my older sister, my younger sister, or my own daughter, ended up like that?

How would I feel?'

A wave of sadness washed over me. I turned to my friend.

'This kind of talk on a night out really kills the vibe, you know.'

Next to us, Duyên lay obediently as she continued cooking, oblivious to our conversation.

A waiter stepped in with a tray on which sat a bottle of champagne and three glasses. He said,

'Esteemed sirs, the lady has arrived.'

Duyên jerked up, alarmed.

'Oh darn! Already?'

The waiter responded.

'Still chatting with the madame.'

'Wait until I'm all the way downstairs before you let her up, okay? Alright, bye for now, brothers.'

Duyên then left with the waiter.

Soon after, the delicate sounds of high heels echoed up the stairs, then stopped at the doorstep. The two of us still stretched out by the lights, I called out.

'We'd love your company, my lady.'

An extended silence. Just as I sat up, the girl gently made her way inside. The moment we could all make out each other's faces, I felt the ceiling collapse, the ground going under, and an abyss yawn wide in front of my very eyes. Judging from the way she froze in place, the girl must've also been just as stunned.

My friend croaked like a toad, managing a singular screech.

'Huyền!'

In a daze, I parroted.

'Huyền! Yes, that's Huyền.'

Meanwhile, Huyền stood stupefied, unable to recognise us. Quý beamed.

'What a surprise!'

I played along.

'Yes, indeed.' I turned to Huyền. 'Huyền, you remember us? Come in, come in.'

Dumbstruck, she said,

'You seem very familiar!'

Through gritted teeth, my friend groaned in French.

'Ah, c'est la vie.'

I stood up and took Huyền's hand, leading her to the sofa. I stopped in my track, unable to take my eyes off her, as my friend Quý anguished over the circumstances of our chance encounter. Noticing the well of sorrow, torment, and surrender in my eyes, Huyền blinked as if blinded by light. Her cheeks were flushed.

I couldn't tell if she recognised us or wanted to hide her embarrassment, but calmly she called out,

'Well, I still have no clue who you are!'

'He's...'

I raised a hand to stop my friend from finishing. If Huyền hadn't remembered, then I wanted her to remain so. If we jumped into introductions now, this merry moment would turn sombre.

'Let's settle down first!' I told Huyền and joined her on the sofa.

I wanted to maintain this silence, so that it might allow new feelings and rare sensations to sink in among us. But it was ripped apart by my friend's audacious outburst.

'Opium! Even opium! Good heavens, I might as well off myself.'

Whether his words were genuine or jocular, a gesture of distress or jest, I didn't want to know, seeing it as outright crass and inapt. I turned to him and frowned.

'Knock it out, you crétin!'

As if catching the French I just hurled at my friend, Huyền seemed fidgety, blinking at me then lowering her head. Her hands, her warm, small, ivory hands, still in the tight clasp of my own.

Life felt like a living hell for me then.

As recent as four years ago, Huyền was still out and about on the streets with her husband, a gentleman whose bountiful dowry had the entire H.G. Street buzzing. I never saw her around since then, and figured she moved to some remote mountain province for her husband's job.

When we were in our prime at sixteen, Huyền was a mere schoolgirl. She was well-groomed, well-behaved, well-raised, the daughter of a judge, the niece of a doctor. All the guys in our class had a soft spot for her, especially Quý, who was entirely besotted. We collectively revered Huyền as the epitome of maidenhood.

Whenever she donned her dainty Kinh hat as she hurried from home to school, Huyền would assume a posture so upright that even the most rogue rascal wouldn't dare come near. Her beauty was of innocence and purity, indicative of her future virtuous wifedom. It was the venerable beauty emblematic of floral fragility, that which made her followers feel uncouth and undeserving; and, if they laid a hand on her, they'd violate a code of conduct and make her beauty vanish into thin air...

Among my schoolmates, as many as thirty were into her, but no one had the balls to confess. Everyone buried their infatuation for her, perhaps out of fear that their thoughts, if uncovered, would expose their idiocy. Huyền's charm was so sublime that even the most stuck-up, big-headed lad to ever live would feel unworthy of her.

Tây Thi, Hằng Nga, Muse, Aphrodite: these are the names people used to call Huyền, besides the name on her birth certificate. As for Quý, he kept calling her 'the lady', as if in a novel. 'The lady's wearing a burgundy shirt today, how marvellous!' or, 'It's official! This year's *prix d'honneur*[1] goes to the lady!'

Every once in a while, Quý would swoon in front me like that without a shred of shame.

In Huyền's presence, we fought to out-dress each other, to flaunt our wealth, to show off our respectable upbringing. Not once did she ever spare anyone a glance; the lady upheld her boundaries, dignified and disinterested as if a married woman with child.

But that didn't deter us from competing, quarrelling,

---

[1] French term for the student with the highest score in the class.

cursing each other out, or moving in packs to sneak on Huyền's brother's friends, who frequented Huyền's place. Fuelled by the nonsense of young blood, sometimes we even made faces at the young chaps who befriended the very man who fathered her. We watched them with disdain, sneered at them with as much contempt as a child could muster, and kept at it until Huyền, having passed the primary school graduation test, eventually walked down the aisle.

After Huyền got married, heartache turned a dozen out of my thirty-ish schoolmates into poets. Still fresh in my mind are Quý's crestfallen face and tearful existential turmoil the day Huyền settled in her husband's home.

And yet now...

Noticing the gloom on my face, Huyền dipped her head... She must've remembered us. I called out.

'Huyền! Huyền!'

'Yes...'

'How full of twists and turns life is.'

'Yes, it is indeed so...'

'Do you recall now?'

'Yes, brother. I think that over there is Quý, who went

to the same school as you...'

Then she stopped short and fixed her gaze on Quý, who was stretching his back sullenly by the tray.

I picked up Huyền's unfinished sentence.

'Back then, Quý adored you very much...'

He feigned elation, a ghostly smile on his lips, and said,

'Thanks, mate.'

I added,

'In fact, even now, he probably still has feelings for you... The day you got married, you had no idea that there was a guy out here nursing his broken heart, so much so that if you ordered him to die, he'd have gladly done so. And yet this is how you've ended up. He must be devastated.'

'Oh brother! This life, this body of mine has nothing to offer for such love! Those who love me will only add to my misery.'

As we were talking, my friend sharply turned his back to us. He had one arm under his head as a pillow, the other draping over his head, while he bent one leg and stretched out the other. If an artist captured his posture now, they could fashion a masterpiece with the bitter text *The Disillusioned* underneath. I told Huyền,

'Let's get on the bed and light some up first.'

'Yes, brother.'

'So you're a dancer now?'

'I did it for some time, but quit a few months ago.'

'Why? Was it no better than this kind of trade?'

Huyền shook her head dejectedly.

'This trade, that trade, they're all the same! I'd rather stick with one...'

Huyền unclasped her shoe buckles and climbed onto the bed. I gestured for her to turn Quý to face us, but she gave me a pleading look of fear, shaking her head. When I pulled at my friend, he resisted, his shoulders as stiff as a log. I snapped.

'Quit it, you git! Turn over, will you?'

My friend wouldn't budge. I had to grab him with both hands. He finally turned over, revealing two trails of tears still moist on his cheeks. Witnessing the solemn air around him, I lost my sense of humour and fell silent. Then calmly I consoled him.

'Get a hold of yourself, man. You know very well that there are times when we need to keep our cool, or else we'll end up the butt of a joke.'

In a pained voice my friend replied.

'You... You can't... You can't understand my torment... You have no idea the extent of my love for her back then, unmatched, unrequited, unspoken...'

Hiccups after whimpers punctuated his words, his despair pierced through me, my stomach ill at ease. My friend continued, sobbing.

'That my life has gone to the dogs is one thing, but how did my most beloved also turn out like this!'

Huyền, too, broke into tears, her voice choked up.

'Thank you... Yes, thank you. Gratitude is all I have now, for I don't know how I can return your precious affection!'

We talked the night away.

***

Upon the birth of his daughter, the father gave a single shrug, grumbling, 'A girl...? What a drag!' The man's sister frowned, 'What a potty mouth! A child is a child, no matter what!' She then visited her sister-in-law in the maternity ward with new cotton facecloths, milk, wine, and plenty of other bits and bobs.

Although a girl, the baby nevertheless grew up in indulgence. She only had to suck, sob, and scream at her mother to change the diaper...

At the age of three, the whole family clamoured to kiss her. Some would peck her until she shrieked and broke into tears, while some wrapped their lips over their teeth to chomp on her podgy arms.

At thirteen, she was often scolded.

Once she turned sixteen, she was still frequently reprimanded by her overprotective family, but her allure began to inspire many young boys to revere her as The Muse. People worried that she would turn corrupt, but no—the young girl remained upright, then got married. Her parents were showered with praise. Word had it that the girl would grow into a cultured wife and committed mother.

Yet, suddenly, one day, they found *that girl* whoring herself. Those who didn't bat an eye muttered, 'What a wretched family.' Those who wanted to get the dirt but hadn't a single clue wagged their tongues: 'It's all because she's corrupt! Even a mother of many can't fully grasp her husband's psyche... That's what she gets for going down the corrupt road. Her life wrecked by her own body.'

And so spiralled Huyền's social standing, or that of corrupt girls like Huyền.

Corrupt?

What were the implications of that word?

What did it mean to be corrupt?

Why did we call it corrupt? How did one become corrupt? If she was corrupt, then should she take responsibility for herself, or did others also deserve the blame?

And why did she become corrupt?

Why did a well-bred girl, who lacked no access to education, end up whoring herself?

'Because she's corrupt.'

'But why is that?'

We nudged those difficult questions into our chat with Huyền. From that night on, the three of us met up many more times. My friend wrote to his family that he fell ill and had to stay in Hà Nội for treatment.

We did our 'homework' on Huyền's corruption...

And Huyền's novel?

Right here.

I - Puberty

Though now a veteran in the business of pleasure, when I had to pen this lowly life of mine, I believed my innocent and unblemished childhood deserved the public's attention and curiosity for the same question that had plagued me for so long: 'How did I fall into corruption?' To the meek mothers, fair fathers, and luminous ladies who may read this memoir, I promise that I'm not playing the believer confessing my sins to some cleric. I won't shoulder all the fault for this filthy life by myself, because the forces that sent me down the muddy path transpired in my years of innocence. I'm not bearing all the blame, because who'd ask that of wide-eyed children? Yet I blame neither life nor anyone for that matter. I did it to myself, and I have to reap what I sow. One should have enough self-respect to own up to their mistakes. As such, to one woman, this memoir can be considered a whore's confession, and to another, a verdict against society. Regardless of reception, I'm certain it'll find a use to reflective souls.

I was born the year Germany declared war on France. By the time I was seven and my hair grew long enough for comb headbands, my older sister had already mastered rice-cooking, while my older brother geared up for school and my mother had just given birth to a girl. A two-storeyed, Western-style building on X Street, my house had a railway for steam trains in the front, and even a flower garden. Every day, I'd wander the streets and play with the other kids, watch the locomotives passing by with wheels that crunched out bright blue flames, fill my pocket with trumpet flowers, fixate on uncles on the street making cigar- and bike-shaped wafers, or study a beggar for hours on end... The heyday of my life! My relatives always cooed at how cute I was, showered me with kisses and money, gave little bites to my cheeks and arms.

Four times a day, without fail, my father would sit imposingly in our black private car and make the journey between our home and his office. Every time his name came up, everyone would call him 'Judge'. My mother tended to the family and gave birth to more children. As I grew up, I learned that my paternal grandfather was once a royal mandarin, and my blood uncle was almost done with his medical degree overseas. Climbing on my high horse, I ignored the neighbourhood kids whose fathers weren't judges, whose families didn't have private cars, and whose clothes couldn't match up to mine. That vanity infected me as a child and incurably afflicted me for the rest of my life, even when I fell into depravity.

Then I started school. Naturally gifted, I was the teacher's pet and the family's golden child. By the time I was fifteen, other girls began to look at me with fear and envy, while the boys plotted to get in my... pants. Puberty, a rotten environment, and unsavoury company, all fused into a flawed education system that eventually threw me to the wolves.

From the outside looking in, people couldn't fathom my rotten environment as the cause. They'd only blame me for being a spoiled and corrupt child. Here was a father with status, a mother with character, a lineage of governance, even a medical doctor in the family, not to mention the fact that education was served to me on a silver platter. Who could say that that was a rotten environment? Forget it. That environment was rotten in petty ways only I would know! Everyone has eyes, but very few truly see; many would hurry to bury anything unsightly that comes their way. They'd be too appalled to bring it up, let alone entertain the thought of curing it.

When I turned eight, while other girls filled their time with snacking, *dolls* caught my attention. My obsession wasn't like that of any other child, who'd beg for a doll only to break it a couple of days after. No, I cherished my doll, nagged my mother to sew shirts for it, cradled it every day, and talked to it as if it were a real person. That was due to the motherly nature the Creator gifted me, I must add. Judging from my character, I could've been a great mother who raised her children with love and kindness. Indeed, though a mere child, I was already curious: 'How does one have a child? When will I have a child?'

When my younger sister learned to roll over, dolls didn't appeal to me anymore. My devotion shifted from dolls to my sister, who could actually smile, speak, and cry.

Then I noticed my mother's belly growing bigger and bigger by the day.

I itched to ask, but for some reason, I hesitated. Some months later, I overheard my father talk about making preparations for my mother's hospitalisation. And he said this with a smile! I couldn't believe my eyes, having seen a rickshaw driver being crushed by a car and hauled into a hospital! My aunt called out then and there, 'About time. Her belly is so big already.' Now that I looked at it closely, my mother's tummy had swollen to such a monstrous size that I had no idea why I didn't notice it before. I asked her.

'Mommy, why is your tummy so big?'

My mother called me over and, gently stroking my head, whispered,

'Because big sis Huyền will have another baby sister soon.'

'Is she here?'

'Right inside my tummy.'

That shocked me even more. I thought the adults were lying to me (because adults would always lie, about anything, at any time). I said curtly,

'You're bluffing!'

My aunt laughed. 'It's true. There's a baby in mommy's tummy.'

I shot back. 'Then what does it suck on? Why is it not crying?'

'I need to give birth to it first!' My mother responded.

I asked again, 'Then where does it come out?'

My mother fell silent. My aunt cackled.

'Through the armpits.'

I believed her (for some reason, despite my belief that adults always lied), and at that moment, my armpits itched as if someone had tickled me. I continued.

'How do you have a baby?'

Before my mother could answer, my father's face darkened.

'Are you still going on about this?' He then turned to me. 'Go play! Go!'

Frightened, I hurried elsewhere.

My curiosity wasn't deterred, but rather fuelled to even greater heights. While I was sold on the armpit birth, I still couldn't wrap my head around why giving birth was a thing to begin with. The unknown confined my mind, only to entice it even more. But, ever since then, no one around me brought up such matters again.

Soon after, as I was passing the time in the back garden one day, I wandered to the chicken coop and came across a hen laying eggs. It stood up, fluffed up its fur; its face paled, the once-red comb, too, then an egg dropped from its tail...

Just then, the old nanny came in to air out some laundry, so I gabbed about what I saw. She told me off, saying that if I watched hens lay eggs, it would give me a rash all over my face. I had no idea what that meant, but I didn't care, anyway. I just wanted to take this chance to get to the bottom of the riddle plaguing my mind. The old nanny mumbled.

'It had its fill of food so it's giving birth, why else! It's giving birth through its ass, how else!'

Her flimsy biological explanations gave me a fright. How come I, after giving myself a pot-belly from eating too much, didn't give birth like the hen? I then got angry that my mother didn't eat well often enough for me to have even more babies.

Then I asked the nanny. 'Why are eggs coming out and not chicks?'

She laughed.

'The eggs come out first, then they hatch into chicks.'

'So my mother lays eggs like hens, too?'

'Yup.'

'Then where do her eggs come from? Like the hens?'

'Through her stomach. Now, belt up and go play, will you!'

From then on, my mother's words held no truth to me.

I thought everything that came out of her mouth was a lie, so whatever she taught me, I'd take it with a grain of salt and follow just for show. My conviction that a full belly would get you pregnant got me a mortifying thrashing.

One day, our family hosted a death anniversary, and the house was packed with relatives and visitors. Among them, there was this gorgeous, young teacher whom I had to address as auntie. She didn't seem to be on friendly terms with my siblings. Down in the kitchen, while watching people prepare for the feast, I heard my sister prattle to my brother that the teacher had a bastard child whom she had to give away. The word 'bastard' flew right over my head; only the fact that she had a child remained. During the feast, when I heard the teacher say, 'The salad is so good, I couldn't help myself from sneaking a few bites earlier in the kitchen,' I immediately responded, 'If you keep sneaking food like that, you'll get so full that you'll give birth and look ugly.'

That was because my mother always looked pale and ugly whenever she gave birth. At the wooden table, some people hid a knowing smile, some glared at me, while the teacher's face turned red. I didn't realise the grave mistake I'd made.

Noticing my sister's tight-lipped smile, I continued. 'My mother is giving birth soon, and I think an egg will come out.'

I didn't expect the instant roar from my entire family. 'Shut your mouth! You wretched child!'

That evening, my father sent me to bed and, with a

bong in hand, prohibited me from repeating such insolent words. He whipped me ten times, each time followed by, 'Understood?'

Of course, I still remember that beating even now. That was the first time my father hit me, and the moment I started to resent him. From then on, I only felt fear towards him—never the same filial love. I didn't know better when I repeated the nanny's words! Under his thrashing, I wanted to snap back, but he forbade me from crying altogether. My early resentment toward my father had irrevocably messed up my learning down the line.

The day after, my sister put me in pretty clothes and took me to the maternity ward, which she called 'the hospital'. The moment I entered, nurses were dashing to and fro. Every once in a while in the next room, my mother would yell, whimper, and shriek, as if pummelled by someone. Then a nurse passed by me, in her hands a bucket with a cotton towel drenched in blood. People congratulated my sister on our mother's new baby boy. I couldn't feel any joy, only dread and disgust. If all that horrible howling was the price for a baby, I swore never to ask my mother for another one. That evening, when I saw the baby, I found out that the nanny lied to me, too. Mother had given birth to a child, not an egg like the hens! And why did adults—all of them—lie so much?

Distraught, I asked my sister again. 'Sis, did mommy give birth through her armpits or ass?'

She hesitated for a while, then said, 'Mommy gave birth through her stomach.'

I was content with her explanation, which I thought was reasonable. Right, how could such a baby crawl through the asshole? He must go through the stomach for sure... 'So when she gave birth, her stomach ripped apart and bled everywhere?'

My sister nodded. That also seemed to make sense, because after every pregnancy, my mother would have to stay in the maternity ward for half a month. Her stomach was probably healing, and her hospitalisation was similar to that coolie driver who had a car accident. My affection for my sister suddenly grew tenfold. She was the only one who was honest with me in this life... And so I thought I had mastered nearly all the mysteries of life. At that point, I still thought we used reproductive organs just to urinate.

But to my disappointment, the cat was soon out of the bag!

Nine years old marked a new chapter of my life. Going to school exposed my naïvety to the many corners of society. Driven by my quest to explore the depths of life's mysteries, I plunged into a world full of stupidity, temerity, monkey business, and gibberish, eventually losing all my inborn compassion. From the birds and the bees to wedlock woes and doing the deed, my brain was basically done in. My desperate need to understand the ins and outs of life's mysteries tuned me to vulgar things that were carelessly discussed around me. I was in a private co-ed school, so I also had some male friends besides female friends. I still hung out with boys without giving it much thought—boys and girls were indistinguishable to me. It also couldn't be helped, as we still borrowed each other's notes and got ready for class together, or hunted crickets, picked flowers, and gathered shoots from red banyan trees together...

One day, in a public garden, I was sitting on a bench with two boys when the topic came up. One boy puffed up his mouth and blew fiercely into the banyan shoot.

I sat there, feigning a distant stare while pricking up my ears at their bickering and taunting.

I interjected.

'Mommy pecks me all the time. How come I'm not pregnant?'

'A peck from your husband is what'll get you pregnant!'

The older boy, pushing the other one, got so angry

that his face turned beet red. I found myself blushing, embarrassed for no reason. Then I wasn't any more, unconvinced by their words. The Creator gifted us that organ with one single use: to urinate; and yet people used it for such bizarre acts? I ventured,

'Really? How do you know?'

'How else? I saw it in broad daylight!'

The other boy pursed his lips.

'You lie!'

'Lie, my ass! I saw it with my own two eyes!'

His confident words brought me seventy percent around, my suspicion reduced to only about thirty. If that were true, then humankind was really rotten. I could not allow my teachers, whom I adored, and my parents, whom I considered as dignified, decorous, and distinguished, to do such disgraceful things. Ngôn, my friend, was perhaps speaking the truth, because if he didn't see it himself, then where else could that lie come from?

However, I chose also to purse my lips.

'Quit it. Ngôn is just making things up!'

The younger boy, buoyed by a fellow doubter, clapped and pointed at his friend's face, rejoicing.

'Eh! Eh! You liar, eh! You stinker, eh!'

Ngôn was upset, maybe less at the mockery but more so at my pout. Furrowing his brows at me as if begging for my trust, he then sombrely spoke to the other boy.

'How about I show it to you?'

Let me remind you that we were in a vast flower garden, in the middle of the French neighbourhood, at the empty hour of one in the afternoon. Above us, a thickset banyan tree eclipsed all sunlight. Amidst this serenity, Ngôn, as soon as he finished speaking, plopped down next to me. On the grass, the other boy sat, equally clueless, motionless, and wordless. Without answering Ngôn, he dilated his eyes wide and mesmerised as if an eager audience awaiting the drama soon to unfold on the stage.

I need not recount what Ngôn did. You can guess for yourself.

It was, at the core, a game to us children. Unlike adults who wanted to hide the bad deed they knew they were doing, Ngôn openly did so in front of other children. The pitiful one here was me, because I had no one to turn to for my curiosity. There were only my mischievous and foolish friends, and without any supervision, I accidentally committed a wretched crime at the age of nine.

That day, my father must've been napping before his afternoon shift, and my mother must've been sitting by the betel nut box. Everyone at home must've thought I was at some friend's house, copying notes, getting homework help, or just studying in general. No one would've expected such a terrible turn of events!

After coming home then going back to class, even well into the afternoon, I still felt a strange sensation in my body. Not only that, I also noticed an unfamiliar fluid leaking from me. Having seen this, I promised myself to start watching out for whatever devilish things were residing in my body...

With no clear instructions from the adults, there was only one way for me to learn: from nature, from the Creator. Just like that, I entered the real world. I began to have a vague idea of why boys and girls were created and why marriage was needed. Once I came to understand better the meanings of vulgarities, the fact that adults used the word for intercourse to swear at each other took me by surprise and mortal shame of all mankind.

How tragic it was that adults like my parents and my teachers, instead of imparting to me the uses and gains of this matter, kept quiet, trashed and thrashed me, and let Ngôn, a literal child, teach me! I decided not to consult adults ever again, because my friends knew enough to 'coach' me. But that was the danger of leaving a child to her own devices, who, at that time, knew not what danger was!

That night, I had a mental breakdown. This feeble spirit of a nine-year-old girl caved in under the thrill of her curiosity and repulsive thoughts... I tossed and turned in bed, one question making rounds in my head: 'Is that all there is to it?' Then I suspected that Ngôn, being only a year older than me, wouldn't have the answer to everything, either.

Shame and fear consumed me. If my parents found out, a brutal beating would await me. What if I just learned my lesson and quit it? Maybe! But easier said than done...! Thought after thought flooded my unnerved mind, nagging, until I somehow drifted off to sleep.

From that day on, I grew self-conscious. I distanced myself from the boys, and steered clear of my youngest brother's lower body parts, which my mother loved dearly, fondled frequently, and even called me over to see sometimes... When my mother held my brother's thing to my face and joked, 'You like this? You like this pee-pee?', I'd run straight out. She'd then compliment me, 'My daughter has matured, she has learned—she has become a very good girl!' I thought I deserved it and so enjoyed every compliment from her.

Three days later, for no particular reason, I went to look for Ngôn. He had fallen sick. His mother, the wife of a civil servant, kept asking me, 'Hey, Huyền, that day when you all went to the garden, did Ngôn pee on any banyan tree?' Her question startled me, but before I could reply, she was already talking to other adults about preparing some cleansing offerings. She then added, 'His fever has had him bedridden for a few days now.'

Unable to meet my friend, I took my leave, dejected. The following days of going to school by myself were terribly lonely.

It was also then that I began to keep track of my hair growth, dreaming of the day I could wear khăn vấn[1]. I kept my face, hands, and feet squeaky clean; I also picked up makeup, though not bold enough to put on powder whenever I pleased. My father remarked contentedly, 'She looks like an adult now!'

After Ngôn got better, he came to school with me every day like always. Whenever we had time, most often on our way back home from school, we'd whisper about nothing but the birds and the bees.

---

[1] A kind of traditional Vietnamese headscarf, worn by both men and women until the 1920s when influences of Westernisation encouraged men to cut their hair short and forgo wearing their hair in buns. During the 1930s-40s, despite widespread campaigns for newer, more 'liberating' hairstyles for women which were only welcomed by younger city girls, many still kept with the tradition of khăn vấn due to its prestige of modesty and respectability.

Once, he recounted in great detail how his parents slept with each other, which he witnessed from the bed next to them. A veil between him and his parents, they didn't know he was awake with the lights on bright the entire time!

At this juncture, I must step back to request that you social crusaders not judge my story as a national concern just yet. Let us take some time to discuss the parents' neglect and the danger in our—Vietnamese families'— messy arrangement of domestic spaces.

I believe that regarding the birds and the bees, or frankly, sex, for children to engage in it out of foolishness is one thing, but the adults themselves are no better. Designating it a dirty thing, they never bring it up; they never bring it up, yet they go at it day in, day out! They rashly go at it in front of the children, who, by nature, will imitate and obsess over it! If that secrecy breeds such harm, then isn't it better to talk about it openly, the good, the bad, and the ugly?

One day not long afterwards, my father gravely called me over in front of my mother. He yelled,

'From now on, you aren't allowed to hang out with Ngôn!'

That scared me out of my wits. My body froze at the

thought of my father knowing all about our sin. If that was the case, he didn't have to beat me to death; my shame would! But alas! I was a clever one! I feigned innocence.

'Dear father, what is the matter? He has been a great friend to me!'

My father glared and slammed the table.

'My word is final. Just stay away from him! No questions asked. You wretched child, trying to talk reason? Shoo, shoo!'

Lowering my head, I quietly stepped away to the room next door. Then, I heard my mother ask.

'What? What's wrong with Ngôn?'

It sounded like my father sighed and took a seat. Shaking his head, he responded, 'Dear me, kids these days have all gone rogue.'

'What happened?'

My father lowered his voice.

'I was just at the clerk's house... He was complaining about Ngôn turning crooked and his family turning wretched because of that...! Then he told me about this thing he caught the boy doing, a kind of self-stimulation too wicked for me to describe to you.'

'Good grief!'

'He beat the boy so bad that I had to step in, or else he'd die.'

'My word! Mercy me! That boy looks like a gift from the gods, a real heaven-sent! Who would've thought he'd be corrupt so soon!'

'And he's only ten. That's how kids are these days. I get chills thinking about it! Our elders were nothing like this!'

'Exactly. Back in the day, kids their age still ran around naked.'

'And now!... The little rascals are too young for this! Modern culture, my ass! He's barred from our family now! Nothing will end well if Huyền keeps mixing with him!'

'Absolutely, who would dare let that devil in their home anymore?'

Having heard enough, I tip-toed out to the garden. Resentment was the first thing I felt. If anything, my parents were as 'corrupt' as us children! Adults did it all the time, but when we did it, that became a sin? Then Ngôn's parents came to mind... How was I supposed to respect my parents now? All adults seemed to me as dirty as Ngôn... On second thought, it didn't feel dirty anymore, because I didn't want what I did with Ngôn to be a dirty thing. Finally, the fear hit me. Every day I worried that Ngôn would get beaten into blowing the gaff on us. I'd kill myself if that happened!

Fortunately, a couple of weeks later, the clerk was sent off to work in Hải Phòng. I never saw Ngôn again.

Ngôn's beatings scared me from even entertaining the thought of playing 'husband and wife' with any other boy. I took secret delight in having dodged a great storm and, since then, tried my best to suppress my pre-puberty urges. I was maturing, after all; I had to have some wits about me by now.

Schoolwork, menial chores, and seeing friends day after day—all this shaped me into a proper and pliant lady, little by little... Until I was thirteen, I never revisited Ngôn's lesson. My shame and fear passed judgement on me, and restrained me from going too far back into that memory.

However, at thirteen years of age, I began my daily fight against lust... The subtle and sweeping growth of every sophisticated organ in my private parts set my body ablaze, even nearly uncontrollable at times. The strangest of all was my first period. I took that chance to ask my mother about the birds and the bees, to which she replied, 'You'll know when you get married'. So you see, my family's entire sex education came down to that one single sentence!

At the age where earthly desires blossomed, this girl was harbouring countless concerns, unable to confide in anyone! Her lips wouldn't crack open, not even with her own mother. Oh misery! Oh calamity! Yet, on second thought, it was hardly any fault of mine. Heaven created me this way. Yes, the Creator had granted us this tedious body, that which sprouted without warning, bringing us not only pleasure and promise, but also agony and catastrophe. I didn't realise then that education was the sole remedy for this crisis. But on Vietnam's soil, who knows when that kind of education would materialise for the good of young people!

During those few years, my mood was god-awful. Without fail, whenever my hands were inactive and my mind idle, I'd think of sex, and worse, lustful desires. This happened only on the inside and at night, however. During the day, when at school, I still dressed with dignity and walked with poise, my gaze unwavering, my expression kept gentle and harmless. Thus, the boys at school often pursued me, dubbing me Tây Thi, The Muse, and many other glittering names.

My mental crisis at fifteen and sixteen was deranged,

debilitating, and disastrous. My rationality stabilised as each year went by; my innate goodness was nurtured every day by books of ethics, abstract and noble ideas, and concerns for my future responsibilities. But alas, the mysterious workings of nature still had the last say! The spring of my youth arrived with unusual vehemence, my flesh seemingly unable to comply with the reasoning of my soul. And then... the lustful thoughts and the unbearable heat of the flesh kept gnawing at my precious sense of shame—something that is indispensable to a woman. Already an albatross around my neck, the weight of my honour was now hanging by a hair. Hearing the unkind words people used to describe adolescence, that inescapable spell of crises, I silently wallowed in shame and disgust. This shame often shifted into resentment, which, from time to time, I would find quite justified, though I couldn't figure out why. It was likely a subconscious arrogance on my part, a wounded ego, the self-justification of those who wished to fall into corruption. Perhaps Christian rhetoric could convey my point more plainly: I was tempted by the Devil with no Angel in sight to heed my cry, to inspire my morals, to console my mind! My parents and teachers had left me to toil this thorny path and pursue this uphill battle on my own. They abandoned me in the thick of a narrow hill slippery with moss and slimy with mud, wedged between steep cliffs and deep caves. While the knowing adults steered clear from me, the ignorant crowd of children seduced me, most of whom were the girls in my class, the children and servants in the house... Whenever topics of copulation between man and woman came up, rather than imparting knowledge about the science of sex, that society would end up fanning my flames.

As such, I knew that this destructive obsession also haunted most adolescents from around nine and ten to fifteen and sixteen years old. They, too, were tormented by the burning desire of their own flesh and confined by the darkness of the unknown; puberty, their innate character, the world around them, all edged them on. The greater their curiosity, the graver constraints they faced, and the graver the constraints, the greater their curiosity. As a result, they got their hands on such erroneous information that the honourable and sensible sensation of pleasure was disregarded altogether. A herd of horses they were, scrambling for scientific knowledge but barely scratching the surface when they collided and collapsed onto each other, then at last, crumbling into bits and pieces...

Adults never taught children going through puberty what they needed to know. Through a stern silence bordering on sacrosanctity, they glossed over the issue of copulation and the anatomy of genitalia! At school, diagrams of the human body explained, with excruciating detail, the eyes, the brain, the heart, the bone, the shoulder, the small intestine, the stomach. Yet no mention was ever made of the reproductive organs, the most necessary organs that ensured the continuation of our species; they created historical heroes and heroines, and orchestrated, organised, and ordained every matter on earth.

Due to adults' hypocrisy and inane sense of shame, children (including me) had to find other ways to educate themselves. Intrigued by a pregnancy, a maternity ward, a wedding, a married couple strolling the streets, children dragged themselves away from adults so that they could naïvely discuss copulation, marriage, love, and so on.

I, myself, had seen children, who were at best twelve years old, innocently debate about love, study and play with each other's reproductive organs, and mimic adults... There were boys, barely thirteen, who spent all their waking hours on those intrusive thoughts, their faces pale and sickly from masturbation.

What a great tragedy for love when the blameless and pitiful youth were falling victim to wicked crimes because of the adults' defective education!

My mental crisis altered my personality. Terrified that people could see through my dirty thoughts, I pulled a veil of innocence over everything I did and said. My sincere, bashful disposition waned with a more frequent use of makeup. My flesh had plumped to perfection, while my body parts filled out, buxom and blossoming. With my period came minor ailments and, upon my recovery, uncontrollable fantasies about men.

Regardless of my resistance, the yearning of my flesh continued to crucify and incite me.

One time, a girl in my class named Ngân broached our shared suffering. She was the most proper and brilliant girl in class, so I cherished her deeply. When she gave good advice, I followed; when she gave bad advice, I copied her all the same. We kept no secrets between us. That day, we were vilifying a girl on the same street for having a child out of wedlock when the topic of love came up. Then commenced our confessions...

'Hey Huyền, let me tell you this—and promise you won't laugh, alright? It's hard for humans to avoid corruption, especially for those in our shoes... But if they have some wits about them, they can protect themselves from harm. For example... We can be corrupt in private. How about we promise to never take a lover? We'll still marry like every other proper person, but in the meantime, we are our own lovers. You with me? A private act that leaves no trace, and we won't have to carry any regret for the rest of our lives.'

She raised her hand, all high and mighty, and added.

'The most beloved lover, one that stays loyal for life and shields us from slander, is this very hand!'

That afternoon marked my induction to a marvellous routine! Ngân also cautioned that I shouldn't be too rough lest I tear my hymen.

I coped with my carnal urges using that method without rest, until I noticed buzzing in my ears, flashes in my eyes, ache in my head, fatigue in my back, and the paling of my complexion by the day.

One time, I confessed my sins to another sister friend. This lady, Văn, was a bona fide pure and chaste maiden. Raising argument after argument, she elucidated the bad karma of masturbation. Should I keep up with that wretched act, soon enough, I'd drain all my strength, my willpower, my dignity, and my vice would be written all over my face. And if that were to happen, I'd be left in the gutter. Then she taught me that copulation must be on the basis of marriage. An act of supreme sanctity— it shouldn't be considered dirty unless it was between an unmarried couple. After lecturing me on legitimate lust and illegitimate lust, she warned me to ignore the dandies' cloying courtship, for their singular goal was to lure us into immorality and satisfy their own sex drive. Finally, Văn gifted me an educational book on men and women, and told me to read it in secret.

And thus I was saved by that astute, once-in-a-lifetime friend. The book I received contained texts and drawings on the genitalia of both men and women. I had secured science. Knowledge relieved me of my once catastrophic curiosity. My wits and reason made their way back to me, and so did virtuous and honourable principles, reclaiming their place from the clutch of lustful thoughts.

***

Love and genitalia

'The Creator gave birth to man and woman in order to prevent humankind from extinction. Copulation is then a given. They call that love. Then where does love come from?

'It comes from the genitalia, which means reproductive organs.

'If thirst and hunger come from the digestive system, then love comes from the reproductive system. The need for consumption is triggered by the digestive system. Those with weak digestive systems do not bother to eat or drink; those with corrupt digestive systems vomit out everything they put in. Love and genitalia work similarly. Those with healthy reproductive organs will experience passionate and pleasurable love; otherwise, it shall go stale.

'Some say: love lies fundamentally within the mind, not the act of copulation.

'Others say: true love has no need for copulation.

'Both are untrue. Copulation is the telos of love. Thus, should a boy and a girl harbour love for each other, they will think about copulation, and when they stop thinking about copulation, they no longer love each other. Henceforth, love requires copulation to sustain its passion, or else it shall dwindle.

'Let us take a look at hermaphrodites. No matter how beautiful, brilliant, or praiseworthy they are, they will never enjoy the love of any mortal. That further proves that genitalia and love are innately co-dependent.

'Therefore, male and female genitalia are precious objects that call for meticulous preservation. If one destroys that treasure to satisfy one's own impermanent, carnal urges, that shall gravely injure both love and our species.'

***

The danger of masturbation and licentious thoughts

'Masturbation is an indecent sexual development that goes against nature and causes great harm. Unwedded boys and girls tend to fantasise about love *in the dead of night. At times like this, the raging fire of lust keeps them so restless and distraught that they resort to using their hands to rub against their genitalia, to alleviate the need to release their vital energy, and achieve a pleasure similar to that of copulation.*

'Those who perform the act will think it is identical to copulation, but in fact, copulation between men and women requires the harmony of yin and yang to facilitate blood flow and prevent hygienic mishaps. In the case of masturbation, only yin or yang energy is present; therefore, blood flow remains obstructed.

'Thus, masturbation has dangerous consequences.

'Men's genitalia will wither as the penis decreases in size and deflects to the side while the testicles become uneven. They will experience erectile dysfunction, spermatorrhoea, and premature ejaculation. Their health will deteriorate and, in some cases, so too will their reason. They will turn mad, or lose their means to bear children.

'And so will women. Other than destroying their genitalia, they will experience red and white discharge, and place their reproductive system in peril; their faces will turn ashen like flowers that are squashed before they sprout!

'What are licentious thoughts?

'That means thinking about lust. Boys who see beautiful girls tend to harbour affection for or an infatuation with her. Should there be an opportunity, each day he'd watch the eastern wall afar, as face dreamt of face and heart wearied heart with toil[1], the image of his lover always in his mind.

'The same goes for girls. Every girl, when idle, will fantasise about her love life and wonder about her significant other, the person with whom she shall join in marriage. Given that natural state of being, no young heart would be able to keep her composure when in front of a brilliant man. As such, licentious thoughts are formed.

'These are normal occurrences for young boys and girls.

'Hence, young people often dream about copulating with each other just like husband and wife. Licentious thoughts have enabled these dreams. This is no less damaging than masturbation. Male genitalia will be afflicted with disease, and, if not cured, end up impotent. Girls may give birth to defective children.

---

[1] Quote taken from Nguyễn Bình's translation of Nguyễn Du's masterpiece, *The Tale of Kiều*, to be published by Major Books, Spring 2025.

'In order to avoid licentious thoughts, boys and girls should study stories of heroes and heroines to cultivate their virtue and set a noble vision in their mind. They should take responsibility and care of their own work to allow themselves no leisure time for licentious thoughts. This period of festering desire proves true that "idle hands are the devil's tools." Thus, train your mind to abstain from condemnable ideas.'

Those passages and the likes exuded a magical power that moved me to the core.

This book on the principles of love has revealed countless truths to this inexperienced brain of mine. The nature of life now stark naked, I no longer harboured misled conceptions of love and marriage. No longer did I perceive the world through an innocent, rose-tinted lens. Huyền could see through it all. Huyền was reaching adulthood, capable of handling the battle on her own. Those pompous beliefs came from my realisation that humans were neither pure nor impure: if copulation was considered dirty by all yet engaged by all, then I should just take it as a natural act. Noble love, ideal love, thoughtful love... such deceitful words youngsters sent in letters to my home had now lost their magic. No longer did they move me in anticipation, nor did my heart skip a beat, especially not when I had instilled in me this truth from the book: *copulation was the telos of love.*

No, Huyền would not remain so naïve that she'd allow life to deceive her. Huyền would never take a lover like most girls, but marry a husband the conservative way. There were youngsters who laboured to fake their mannerism as courteous, amorous, decorous, committed, untainted, and cultivated, and flooded Huyền's home with passionate, burning, and poetic letters. Yet they'd never distract Huyền from this mundane truth: it was all so that they could sleep with her! Out of suspicion of everyone's honesty, this Huyền dared to take pride in the fact that she broke innumerable hearts on purpose.

Now capable of condemning my licentious thoughts as shameful, I felt my spirit growing stronger, enough to restrain the trembling of my flesh and break free from the temptation of every evil influence that surrounded me.

I also found myself pure, though not necessarily innocent. Although my mind had suffered the electrifying stimulation of countless lewd and ruthless tempests, I still considered myself untainted. A funny idea popped into my head: if poets ruled that a pure woman must never fall shameful hostage to licentious thoughts and fantasies fuelled by youthful physical arousal—yes, if a pure woman must serve as the mysterious woman created by nature while also shunning the ordinary act that brought her to life, then those poets would never find a pure woman in this entire world! Why was I pure? Just because I was still a virgin, and I didn't have a lover. And a woman having these two traits was already pushing your luck!

When I managed to be at peace with myself, life appeared wonderful, worthwhile, and overflowing with happiness... I had outlined for myself an itinerary: marry a husband on equal footing, be dedicated to one life partner, observe the *one wife one husband* rule until the end of time, and become a humble wife and filial daughter-in-law. 'A happy family'—those three words articulated to me an unimaginable, peaceful pleasure.

Thus, for exactly one year, I indulged in books and home economics. Those terrifying moments of depravity, even if I wanted to, could never resurface.

As I tamed myself, the public also spared no lenience for the corrupt. Back then, a despicable incident happened at a girls' school: a dormitory supervisor madame caught two schoolgirls masturbating with each other using a rubber tool... The news caught fire all over the country! For quite a while, at the mention of the New Woman movement, equality, or feminism, people would bring up what those schoolgirls did. The upper-class intellectuals who gathered around a party table, the rickshaw drivers who pulled empty rickshaws on the streets, the servants who huddled at water fountains—from high to low, from young to old, across every single social class, if they ran out of things to talk about, everyone would bring up that scandal as a conversation starter. An entire society shared one tongue, lapping up the outrage, deriding that act of masturbation. The first time I got wind of their blistering commentary, I was paralysed with fear, as if the convicted criminal had been me. Trembling, I recalled my mistakes of the past, then quietly celebrated my luck for having dodged a bullet from the public while still retaining my honour. Since then, I understood the menacing power of public shame as necessary to orient man's heart and common sense. Other people's mishaps were my cautionary tales. Even though I escaped the public's arrow, I nevertheless became a bird afraid of its own shadow...

And that wasn't the end of it! Society had an endless supply of nonsense. History was just a series of extended dramas on loop. Last month, a noble lady was stripped naked by her lover in a brothel. Last week, someone showed up to a married woman's house and cussed her out for seducing another's husband. The other day, a lady had a baby out of wedlock with her personal driver. Today, two esteemed educators committed adultery. What would tomorrow bring—and then the day after? I chuckled to myself at those pitiful people, who perhaps had jeered at others' sinful deeds only to end up sinful and ostracised just like them. Unable to keep up, I simply went along with the public and pointed fingers at others...

After I received my primary school certificate, my father deemed that was enough education for a girl and took me out of school. As I grew, so did my value in other people's eyes, no matter how little. The world around me praised my beauty and admired my docility. Diligent labour, modest manners, seemly speech, moral conduct: having attained all four virtues, I sheepishly made my entrance into society. I acquainted myself with women of great status and prestige: the wife of this man, the daughter of another man, women who were born with silver spoons in their mouths or taking half a day to powder their faces. Young lords and noblemen flooded to befriend my brother. Matchmakers fired information back and forth... My father turned cocky, and so did my mother, which excited me greatly. I was only sixteen!

While I revelled in familial bliss and the vainglorious title—The Muse—that the infatuated secretly called me, the life of this reformed society wreaked vile influences that wrecked my morals.

Society was, lo and behold, even more frightening than puberty. At that time, a tempest swept through our society. The materialist movement emerged in the guise of deceitful nouns: progress, reform, a new way of life... Its special power was near-universal, delusional magic. The tempest wiped clean old habits and disciplines. Materialism turned upside down the former order of an idealist society. There emerged a generation of foul reporters and writers who caged up their wives, children, and sisters in closed off chambers, all while hollering their throats off, imploring other people's wives and children to clamber out into society. They were to live the new life of marketplaces, dances, and trendy clothes that increasingly revealed body parts that a woman should conceal. Journals that didn't advocate for modernity and didn't butter up to those in power would take turns digging their own graves. Nationalism and socialism: dead in a ditch. Those who didn't blindly chase after materialism would be called asinine, archaic, and a waste of space. Newspapers were packed with discussion forums on ways to pleasure the flesh. If they didn't acknowledge materialism, young people had no other ideologies to follow. Literature and the arts became mere tools to exalt servitude to the Lord of Lust.

Dance parlours wrecked domestic happiness, turned women into whores, lodged horns on men's heads or drove them to scorn their wives. They handed brothel owners the jackpot, and crowned 'drug dealing kings' left and right...

Women's outfits revealed, by the day, a bit more thigh, a bit more ass, a bit more tits... In cities, you could find carnal thrill and temptation from Eros in every nook and cranny. Meanwhile, villages remained impoverished, neglected, polluted, as the epidemic of despotic landowners, superstition, bribery, and illegal alcohol dregs continued their rampage...

When I closed my eyes and followed this new life, I still thought that that was the modern and civilised thing to do. When I sobered up, it was too late.

When I realised my mistake, I was already... a whore!

II - Into The World

These were all scornful arguments against the pompous, the wanton, and the extravagance of a depraved society nearing its end. Here, ninety percent of people mistake the meaning of human life and virtuous ideals for simple material satisfaction and physical fulfilment—not to mention immoral behaviour, the lust, the speech, the fakery, the snobbery. Yes, this condemnation of such a wretched state of affairs is coming from someone like me, the kind that went to waste and yet was exalted by the progressives as a pioneer in the Westernisation movement. I was considered an exemplary individual of thrill, energy, novelty, an experimenter in the new wave of social trends, dancing, socialising, the kind that broke the door to her boudoir to join 'society' while mouthing slogans of liberation and equal rights. Surely, many would freeze in awe and ponder how this irony came to be.

But woe, this turn of events is to be expected, even so ordinary that it deserves none of your curiosity. If a woman who cheated a lover came to regret it, then to her, that lover would appear to be the most detestable thing in the world. Like me, who's been through the hands of hundreds of thousands of people, she'd come to recognise the value of being human. She'd turn to resent the wanton, the pompous, and the reckless with a decidedly more intense passion than that of moralists demoted to degenerates. Only those devastated by love know to fear it; only those whose riches rival none know the mundanity of silver; only those who have reached the zenith know the tedium of reputation; and only those who've lived a blissful life know by heart the incomprehensibility of happiness. But what do I know? Already people are protesting that a whore like me has no right to speak like that and shouldn't think like that, so what's the point of me talking anymore? We learn the ropes only through experience. An experienced woman is a ruined woman. That's irrefutable. Unlike innocence, the cause of foolishness and depravity, having experience is an abhorrent thing that strips the woman of her right to impart her wisdom and help the inexperienced majority.

Given the status quo, should I try to overcome the malignant prejudice that streetwalkers shouldn't discuss women's ethics? So that those dreamy, happy-go-lucky young girls would walk themselves towards love and sin, one step at a time, bashful yet brave and eager, toward that place of death oozing with poetic delight and promise of absolute physical euphoria? Toward that which merciless masters claim as progress, joy, liberation for equal rights, and civilisation? Or should I keep my mouth shut?

Should I try to save anything that could still be saved? Should I just let this wave of materialism sweep the majority of girls into debauchery, so that it wouldn't be a bad thing for me to be a whore when everyone was?

But woe is me! I don't think like most streetwalkers, who believe that if we can't amount to anything, then no one could maintain their honour. Even after whoring herself out, Huyền had yet to figure out the ultimate conclusion about life. She was unable to enjoy a whore's thoughtless and filthy life, bursting with repugnant and reluctant pleasure! She still wants to use whatever is still usable in her soul to help others. She still wants to resist the movement! She doesn't understand that the fragile will of an individual has no chance against a movement. Yes, if the young Huyền could've resisted the movement, would she still have ended up like this? Anything that rises against a movement will be seen as degenerate, outdated, and ludicrous, even though it was rational, moral, and ethical. Unable to differentiate right and wrong, I made mistakes, like sheep that inevitably return to their herd, and moths to a flame. I, too, caved to mainstream pressure.

Back then, women's issues were on the rise across the nation. Never before were women so pampered and pandered to. All the journals wanted to break down the boudoir door and let women onto the streets... Intellectuals elucidated to us the new way of life that was more worth living, a life of advocacy for our individual rights rather than the old routine of sacrificing for our families. Flaunting fancy names, those intellectuals cunningly exploited literature and the arts to reform the hems and cuffs on women's clothes! Makeup methods like lipstick and blush were as worshipped as war heroes. Bootlick! That became the motto of those who wished to be exalted to greatness. Dance parlours opened by the hundreds. Publishers only printed books on cavalier girls at work. Photo studios exclusively hung pictures of 'women socialising' at markets and horse races.

Little did anyone know that simple stagnancy was enough to cause extinction. A faithless, uneducated nation without any ideals to worship behaved like a bunch of conmen lured by a rhetoric of mystified nouns, heedlessly blowing up this already corrupt and crippling life by plunging headfirst toward materialism. When everyone tended only to their lust, the individual became divorced from the community. Under the delusion of advancing toward civilisation, an entire society couldn't fathom the possibility of having fallen into the trap of the Lord of Lust. Even those who had a brain were bewitched to reject centrism and embrace the call for comprehensive reformation. How catastrophic these misconceptions in gullible minds.

At first, my corruption took harmless forms, such as my white trousers, white teeth, leather wallet, and my frank conversations with men or a few 'boyfriends'. One day I'd go to a movie, the next day a market, the day after a ballroom dance. Technically, only foreign wives or women whom society loosely called 'romantic' would do this. And yet I had to get my white trousers tailor-made, just because my girlfriends had spurned the darker-coloured ones. All day, every day, they took turns to jeer at me; it didn't take long for me to surrender. Remember: white or black, by itself, neither stained nor raised one's dignity. At the same time, my corruption did begin with a pair of white trousers[1], and no, I wasn't exaggerating. It remoulded my view of clothing and mannerisms, and unveiled a sense of liberation, socialisation, aesthetic inclination, and every other bad habit hidden in the word 'modern'. If a young lady boldly struck a conversation

---

[1] Related to the 'Modern Woman' movement, the newspaper *Phong hóa* shared women's opinions: 'We prefer the soft, cool white silk trousers over the thick, coarse black ones, where one cannot tell what filth is on them, yet the elders call them clean because they are black.'

with a man, how could that be called corrupt? And yet this inconsequential banter caused endless adultery and unwanted pregnancies! Corruption crept on us in a myriad of forms: today we might have a formal conversation, tomorrow we might feel faintly each other's absence, the next day we might find ourselves in love, then sooner or later, we'd be making a pledge of loyalty, sending letters back and forth, then one day, out of nowhere, a smile, a glance, a kiss, a sigh... going from those little gestures to lovemaking was only a matter of time. That should suffice to explain the public's surprise every time an otherwise honourable woman cheated on her husband, or to address those modern girls who so desired to challenge the no touching rule between men and women with this silly argument: 'Men and women don't sleep with each other immediately as soon as they make contact!' Dear me! Looking back on my life, I'd seen countless women successfully maintain their virtues because they'd never taken those dark-coloured trousers off!

The first time I sneaked by my father while wearing white trousers, my heart was beating out of my chest. He glared and called me over: 'You whore! Did I give you permission to dress like that?' Before I could muster the courage to talk back, my mother joined in: 'Who'd marry a business family's daughter with that kind of get-up?' Fortunately, just then, some of my aunts on both sides of my family were also there. They leaned modern, so some protested against my father, while others smiled jeeringly. After they accused him of being austere, outdated, inane, an aunt gently told him: 'What does it matter, that trifle? Everyone's like that everywhere you go now. If you ban those trousers, Huyền will fall behind the times.' With my father expressing his contempt for women through silence, I managed to escape his admonition. I still got the side glance since then, but that was more bearable than mockery from my peers, so I never backed down in front of my parents. As time went on, the more they complained, the more inured they became, and eventually, no one bothered me any more.

Having conquered the white trousers, I also befriended a few rich girls who exclusively donned modern clothes. They had broken the trust of many relatives and close friends who considered white trousers the epitome of corruption. Now, if those people weren't so aggressive and instead talked to me with more moderate, centrist views, perhaps I wouldn't have strayed so far... But alas, their radicalism only convinced me of their hopeless degeneracy, and thus their valuable advice fell on deaf ears. From one's hostility to another's apathy, not to mention my own ego, I distanced myself from close ones to chase after a new tempting society. And so... today I'd take my photos, tomorrow I'd develop them, in the morning I'd drop by the tailor, at noon I'd enjoy some live music, in the afternoon I'd take more photos, in the evening I'd return one lady's favour, tomorrow I'd host a feast for another new friend, then every once in a while, I'd go to a market or a meeting in a literary coterie. It didn't take long for me to bury my womanly virtues and domestic prowess and transform into a modern girl to be reckoned with. My parents' reproach, advice from the ones who remained close to me, people's overt and covert criticism, everyone was wasting their time flogging a dead horse... My life revolved around the fantasy of a significant other like in the novels, a marriage out of love, a beautiful husband who grew up in riches and knew to treat his wife like those in the West... which was no different from most modern girls!

Besides... , I sighed out of fatigue, and shrugged...

Backlash from conservatives only fired my conceit and confidence, because their accusations of me being 'romantic' and 'corrupt' had no factual basis. I hadn't fallen in love with anyone, and neither had I lost my virginity. The more they tried to warn me, the more hostility I harboured. Soon enough, they let me be and do whatever I wanted.

Not only that, my father also changed out of the blue. The more upright he once was, the more frivolous he became. Almost every night, he'd go out until three in the morning. No one knew if he was gambling or sleeping around, but likely both. Because of that, my mother often wallowed in self-pity, her figure thinning, her health dwindling, her face more and more haggard by the day. It then dawned on me that if young people didn't corrupt themselves a bit while they still had the chance, but waited until they were married and with children to 'break the vows', that would be a catastrophe that even the Heavens could not salvage. Those people would have no qualms about abandoning their wives and children; their families could crumble right in front of their eyes and they'd watch with crossed arms. My mother was the conservative type, the type to grit her teeth and suffer rather than complain, so my family maintained our blissful façade. But a conflict swept under the rug was a ticking time bomb. The longer the delay, the more calamitous the outburst. I despaired at how things had turned out this way for my family, and my respect for my father had vanished altogether.

I could still recall that evening of pouring rain—oh, how ironic! My mother was crying her eyes out while holding the baby, my sister was bickering with the servants in the kitchen, my brother was putting on his jacket and hat to hang out with the rascals and abandoning his studies, and my father was leaving in a car with his old geezers, squandering away the family fortune. All the while, I focused on writing a French composition describing a happy family where the father was reading the newspaper, the brother was studying at his desk, the baby was playing quietly, the mother was knitting a jumper, while I was completing my homework, and so on...

This evening's scene replayed day after day, until my father admitted to my mother that he'd made a singer pregnant, then they fought again and again and, at last, my father triumphantly brought his mistress home. A few days later, unable to stand the eyesores, my mother and the younger children evacuated to the countryside. From then on, my older sister ended up a servant and my brother also turned corrupt, while my father only had eyes for his lovely mistress; as for me, I became a little more 'modern'. As my youth fervently bloomed amidst the crisis, the coincidental nature of life had led me to Nguyễn Lưu.

He was one of my older cousins, the son of an aunt on my mother's side. His parents were tradespeople in Lào Cai. After obtaining his primaire élémentaire[1] certificate, Nguyễn Lưu returned to Hà Nội to attend l'enseignement

---

[1] Primary school

secondaire[1]. He was renting another place before moving to my house so that he and my older brother could be study buddies.

Nguyễn Lưu was a young man of many good traits and very few vices. The complete opposite of my brother's friends who were usually lazy, frivolous, stuck-up, lauding wooing tactics as heroic, Nguyễn Lưu exuded a superior aura with his remarkable diligence, not to mention his distinct integrity that turned a deaf ear to racy matters. Did I perhaps love him? No, it was respect, mixed with a bit of a good impression, but not quite love yet. I knew loving someone from the same bloodline was taboo. So... did he love me, then? That I couldn't figure out, even though I desperately wanted to and paid the utmost attention to his every move. A boy and a girl under the same roof: since we were related by blood and cared for each other, we could converse freely. Our closeness opened up opportunities for love to tease us like a game of peek-a-boo. I didn't know for sure whether Lưu, deep inside, was truly besotted with me in a silent, spiteful way, but I knew for a fact that Lưu cared for my virtues no less than a jealous husband, even more invested than those responsible for my well-being.

He furiously objected to every gesture of mine that

---

[1] Secondary education, junior high school

he thought was an affront to modernity. From tender warnings and figurative insinuations to a passive-aggressive and threatening voice, step by step, Lưu intervened in my romantic schoolgirl life, or tried to isolate me from my peers, those modern girls whom Lưu claimed as corrupt.

After I went on a trip far away, or intimately bantered with my brothers' friends who frequented my house, Lưu's face would darken. His expressions and gestures were enough to expose his jealousy and the true extent to which our familial bond had grown. Yet, no one raised an eyebrow at those behaviours. People had the guts to believe that once related by blood, you couldn't 'fall for' each other.

One day, I chanced upon an envelope in my mirror comb set. Peeling it open, I saw a strange letter, typed on a typewriter, with neither the date nor the receiver's name, or even the sender's signature. The letter solemnly discussed love as if a treatise or translated from some textbook. It went something like:

You should never make a vow. Yes, you should fix it in your mind never to make a vow. Once the flesh has shaken man's heart, he shall promptly disregard sacred and sincere words he once swore by the mountains and the seas. Thus, regret toward the vow shall poison even the most tender of pleasures in the world. Vows are utterly useless and invariably risky.

***

Among all of humans' desires, only love can grant us the most pleasure. However, there exists a prejudice that only men have the right to pursue that desire without devaluing himself; in fact, oftentimes, that desire even earns them immense influence. On the other hand, once a woman loves to the point of entrusting her entire body to us, she deserves our devotion; yet, we come to disdain her or render her dirty by broadcasting her defeat.

That is the trait present in every single man. Men devote their lives to moaning and groaning about feelings they do not harbour, and conjure up schemes to win over women who want to resist them. The Creator has made men so ungrateful and immoral that they continue to carry out their destructive imperative without sparing a single thought for the miserable tears of gullible women.

I finished reading it. While I did find it funny and entertaining, I also felt bothered. What was the intention of the person who wrote it? Who was it, anyway? To admonish me like that, this person must be looking down on me as if I was nearing corruption... Why, this Huyền has no need for anyone's admonition, and neither would she forgive anyone who dared commit such an audacious and insolent act. Oh, the ego, the wounded ego; even worse, the wounded ego of a stubborn young woman of the most self-centred kind, the corrupt one!

After great pontification, I figured only Lưu could've been the 'culprit' of that letter, so I planned to hunt him down for clues whenever I had the chance.

One noon, with no one in the house and Lưu sitting with his face glued to the French maths textbook, I sneaked up next to him and placed the letter in the middle of the table. An honest to a fault man he was, as soon as Lưu saw the piece of paper, his face fell. That alone indicted him; otherwise his curiosity would've urged him to pick up and read the paper.

I sat facing him and asked gently.

'Why did you put this letter in my comb set?'

Without any time to prepare, Lưu, taking in my composure, had no chance to deny, only to find a way to explain himself. After what seemed like forever, he finally stammered out an answer.

'I translated it from a Western book... figured it'd be helpful for you... if you read it.'

My face hardened; I pouted my lips, my voice snide.

'You think I'm corrupt now, don't you?'

'I... don't think it, but I fear it terribly.'

'Then that means you're looking down on me! Who do you think you are? What right do you think you have?'

At this, Nguyễn Lưu ducked his head in shame for a long while, then lifted his face to stare straight at me with the eyes of a madman. He scoffed, choked, then sobbed some more, before he finally said with conviction:

'Right, I have no right, I have zero right! You're just a cousin. But... if you've gone corrupt, then I'll be the most heartbroken.'

What a slippery slope. It was too late for regret. If I hadn't initiated that interrogation, Lưu would've never, under normal circumstances, been so honest and bold as to proclaim his love for me. Because if Lưu dared to openly declare his love for me, that'd be reckless of him, and our relationship would be a filthy affair no less reprehensible than incest. A learned person would never suddenly express his inner feelings like that, if not for some extreme influences.

Now, not only did Lưu feel no shame uttering those words, but I also found his confession natural, justified, and even pitiful. I wanted to stop him and beg him to shut his mouth, yet my throat closed up. Still upset, Lưu continued to grumble.

'Yes... I might as well bite the bullet and bare my soul to you now! You... you have no idea...'

Then he stopped, perhaps searching for a literary expression, some charming nouns, that could thoroughly convey his ideas. Taking my chance with this silence, I tried to calm myself and said,

'You shut up! Just shut up, I beg of you.'

Lưu persisted.

'I'm telling the truth. I've... I've been in great pain! Oh Huyền, you... you have no idea that I'm the most miserable man on earth for loving you... a hidden... disappointing love... for however long... I've planned to live with this pain... to love you in the dark... you who will become a refined wife and dutiful mother... and live in happiness... with another husband... who deserves you... who isn't me. And yet you're always so romantic, so modern!... I can't keep it in anymore! I resent the Creator for our blood relation, for obstructing my love for you... my future as your groom... Now I must suffer so... Huyền...! Huyền, oh Huyền!'

His words tumbled out like a turbid stream, tidal

waves in between dead silences; they wrapped over Lưu like a magic spell and made this bleak tragedy even more demoralising. And so, I was done for!

My heart was pounding in my chest, my limbs quivering as if hit with a cold breeze. As I almost burst out crying, Lưu's tears triggered my own to pour down like an uncontrollable flood. Hit with a dizzy spell, I felt as if I was about to trip and fall from a high building down to the ground.

It wasn't the first time the call of love reverberated in my ears. The youngsters who courted me also had all sorts of tricks up their sleeves, though none actually moved me. Their laughter, glances, jokes, ornate letters were doused in lies; they only maddened me and reduced them to an obnoxious bunch in my eyes. And yet, on the other hand, Lưu... wooed girls with his honesty, his pain, and his tears; in this situation, no woman would've been able to keep her composure!

Lưu plastered his face to the table and sobbed for a while, then stood straight up and spoke in a firm, solemn voice.

'Well, my apologies to you, cousin. My bad, my lady. Do forgive me, yes, I do beg that you ignore what I just said. We're already cousins, so if you won't forgive me, then please keep quiet about what happened, in case of outsiders... even if they're...'

At this, I stood up, completely out of it, and quietly left the room. I halted every three steps. I wanted to console Lưu but didn't know how. Genuinely speaking, Cupid's bow had struck the epicentre of my heart, and I was thus beyond saving. Never mind forgiving him; I wanted Lưu to keep talking, to keep violating that mistake that was oh so deserving of forgiveness, so deserving of love, so that it'd all be worth the risk. Lưu's words of despair both pained me and pleasured me splendidly. Lưu's pain? Why, what else could it be but my happiness!

In that moment, I experienced an array of peculiar poetic delights as though in a novel. My suffering came with great pleasure no different from those protagonists in romance stories where the woman was showered with endearment, reverence, and obedience as if she were an empress in a court, where her courtiers had the sole purpose of cultivating love and pleasure.

I stood there for a long, long time. Though I dared not turn back, I lingered to see if Nguyễn Lưu had anything else to say... But he'd fallen into deep contemplation, perhaps out of regret, or hesitation... Thus, I slowly made my way downstairs.

Ever since that day, my mood underwent unfathomable swings. I was moping all the time. I didn't join those fun hangouts with my lady friends, the kind of activity that Lưu disliked. Unable to be honest with myself, I unconsciously obeyed Lưu's words like a meek wife who, afraid of losing my husband's affection, was constantly scheming plans to set up the mood for love. Lưu and I, we did our utmost to steer clear of each other. But the farther we ran from love, the faster it chased after us! Pain, when escalated to an imminent hazard, resembled a burgeoning balloon that'd pop sooner or later... But the brain's rationality could not compete once the heart decided to claim language for itself.

So here was someone who took matters seriously, loved me in secrecy, only wished for me to protect my purity in all aspects, and yet forced my hands into filth like those of a person without a conscience. Still, Lưu didn't have a mean bone in his body to begin with. For him and me to engage in dirty acts would surely surprise and baffle many. And yet life was indeed that baffling.

I must emphasise that throughout that upsetting series of events, ever since I saw through Nguyễn Lưu's feelings, I devoted my pure, whole heart to him and him only. Despite knowing full well the taboo of this new love affair in my fantasy, in a moment of consideration, I decided to discard my reservations and distance myself from moral teachings of the past. While Nguyễn Lưu didn't come from an affluent family and had yet to achieve a prestigious position in society or demonstrate that he'd love his wife like a Western or modern man, his anguishing love was touching enough to balance out the rest. Anywhere, anytime, no matter what I did, whenever my mind idled, I instantly pictured a happy family with the two of us, the air around us charged with pleasure, the space around us elegantly decorated like other young and humble couples. I could've wished for cars, high-rise buildings, flocks of servants; my social presence could've been defined by parties and festivals day in and out, yet I would've contented myself with a small room, a mediocre set of furniture, a husband who made just enough to scrape by, and a few friends who didn't know much about dance parlours and markets. That kind of life felt good enough, because life without love was a life not lived, and love without sacrifice was a love not valued. Honestly, I thought I was 'sacrificing' plenty for Lưu. If we listened to public opinion, surely I could've married a wealthier husband, no?

Yet, after drowning myself in deceitful literary expressions, I couldn't escape from the truth, that disastrous truth... We were cousins! A love of sacrifice, modesty, and happiness, such honour was no match for this dreadful stain: incest. That thought sent me spiralling in despair and agony. I had no care for the world, not even for my meals, blanking out like a madwoman most of the time.

Snapping out of it, I thought: 'The bubble's burst. Why bother brooding over it and fantasising about it?' But then I countered myself: 'True, but fantasising about that happiness doesn't hurt me or anyone else, does it?' Love was still lurking around me, waiting for its chance to tempt and egg me on...

In contrast, novels offered a completely different world and society. A woman with a bastard child? She was a martyr for love. A whore who slept with different guys every day then died young from diseases? She was a romantic modern girl, her devotion to love enticing poetic thrill... A noble lady sneaked out to meet with her lover and died from love? That was a poetic love affair, an epic historical tragedy. A woman who left her husband because he was a coward and his family backward? She was leading the women's liberation movement to seek individual happiness! Society not only acknowledged those women, but even encouraged and endorsed them. That was in fiction. In real life, if a girl did anything like that, everyone would be on her case, criticising her for being corrupt, promiscuous, a man-chaser... What a rotten disparity. Why did they validate it in fiction only to reject it in real life? Sure, they could say life wasn't fiction, but under other circumstances, they would praise how 'true to life' those novels are. What an alarming and unsettling load of nonsense. Once society looked at it differently, they'd surely turn against some poor girls who made a few mistakes here and there. Those who misconstrued fiction for reality—or reality as fiction—always made up the majority. And if we really thought about it, it wasn't their fault alone!

With that context elucidated, you'll be able to follow the path of my future downfalls.

**

Paul Sanh wore a luxurious Western suit, his black hair slick with wax, ending in loose curls the way philosophers styled theirs. When he shook my hand, I was hit with a puff of perfume. More simply dressed, Mai Thiên Tố had on a white pair of glasses, his skin pearly white with powder, and his lips bright red like a woman's—his only noteworthy features. Among the women, Huỳnh Liên sported a gaudy yellow shirt with Johnny collars, the hems lined with ruffled elastic that made her look like an ultramodern golden oriole. The other two women's clothes appeared more refined at first glance, but the trousers were made from flimsy Shanghainese crêpe. Underneath were groin-grazing shorts that flushed their skin in cherry blossom pink and revealed the curves of their inner thighs... Everyone had their hair up, wore Huế-inspired bracelets, painted hearts onto their lips, and powdered their faces in terracotta, Charles IX dancing shoes on their feet. With pencil-drawn eyebrows whose tails ran upward all the way to her temples like those of seasoned actors in Chinese classical dramas, Huỳnh Liên had the unflinching and unabashed demeanour of a dance girl. Bích Ngọc, the fairest of all, seemed quite Western: her body voluptuous, her eyelashes curled like those of movie stars, her gaze a sheen of dreaminess and mystique, her pupils a velvety black.

The room was also strangely decorated. Chairs and tables were lined up next to each other and along all four walls, leaving the centre vacant. Photos of nude beauties from the West and movie stars filled up the walls. In the farthest corner, another half-room separated by a partition. Through the thin shade, I caught a glimpse of a bed, a study desk, some cloth hangers... Wondering how a schoolgirl's house could look like a schoolboy's hostel, I asked Ngân:

'Between those two, who's the lady of the house?'

My friend answered with the utmost nonchalance.

'This house belongs to the boys. These girls come here just for fun.'

After pouring me some water, the boys invited me to try premium Western candies and British cigarettes, seemingly indicating that making my acquaintance would reinforce the girls' acceptance of them as male friends. This was basic social etiquette, and more importantly, pure friendship. With a closer look, though, I noticed that there wasn't only companionship here, but also romance. The giggles, the glances, the subtle backhanded remarks, oftentimes coloured with jealousy, sufficed to expose these youngsters' exploitative friendships as an excuse to screw around. While more or less under the influence of modernity myself, I still couldn't believe for the life of me that men and women would become intimate without any impure motives.

At first, being around the most progressive individuals in society made me feel self-conscious and ashamed of my inferiority. Like a poor person writhing and flinching away from a crowd of rich people, or a less-educated person standing amidst accomplished men of one credential after another. Then I felt a sense of regret. If Lưu knew I was loitering around a place like this, his adoration for me would surely turn to contempt. At that thought, anger overcame me. I ended up here, mingling with people from whom I should've distanced myself, because Ngân lied to me.

Those people took my silence as me being cocky. I realised that to new people, arrogance was a useful weapon to compel their respect, because even if they didn't know me, they'd respond to my high and mighty attitude with caution first. Indeed, it didn't take long to humble the entire room as everyone scrambled for ways to flatter my ego. After half an hour, we grew so close that my apathetic and pompous attitude earlier seemed quite awkward!

As expected, dancing began to come up in conversation.

It turned out that these students didn't rent this private room to study, but to dance.

'Our old-school parents would never understand the artistic value of dancing, so why should we bother explaining ourselves? We'll do our thing, and they'll die from old age anyway...'

'That's right! The ones living in the future will be us, not them! Our parents will bite the dust sooner or later, but we'll be here for a long time to come! Right, sister Bích Ngọc?'

'Very much so, sister Huỳnh Liên. I feel so démodé not knowing how to dance at parties and whatnots...'

'Heavens! If even us two don't know how to dance, then are we back in... in General Cao Biền's time?'

'No way! Emperor Gia Long would be more like it.'

'I think so too, but the parents at home keep telling me dancing is promiscuous. Oh how my blood boils!'

'Oh! Oh! What bull! So Europe has been promiscuous for the past thousands of years, then?'

'Pipe down! Everything basically boils down to this: our parents are at least forty, fifty years old already; if they danced like us, that'd be so disgraceful! No wonder they tear into us for being loose! Those green-eyed folks...'

'True! Let's have our parents try dancing! They'll be hooked in no time! It's not that easy to act loose around here... One listen to that trumpet line and I'm gone...'

'My brother Thiệu Tố, you must get this in the news...'

'My dear lady, unfortunately, I am only a poet.'

'Besides, despite how it looks, there's nothing promiscuous about this! Our parents just won't allow it because they never got to... essayer quelques pas[1].'

Amidst the group's debate on dancing, a young man walked in. Another rowdy round of introductions. Then more half-finished sentences, more secret gestures, coupled with the usual cacophony whenever someone new arrived.

Paul Sanh turned on the record player. Ngân and I sat still, watching three pairs dancing under the guidance of the newly arrived young man, who was a dance professor.

---

[1] My English translation of this phrasing: Bust a few moves.

That was my introduction to dancing... In front of my eyes was clearly a scene of unrestrained debauchery for those involved, and erotica for those watching. And yet they insisted it wasn't loose. Was it because they saw it as mere art without impurity? I asked Ngân if she knew how to dance, to which she blushed and admitted that she had managed to learn a piece. In the few months that we hadn't seen each other, she'd already snuck out for dancing lessons by herself.

When they put on a second record, Ngân stood up and said to me,

'Hey, let's try dancing to a song!'

I shook my head, but she persisted.

'Just give it a try! It'll be loads of fun. If you can dance, just listen to the music. It'll be like walking on clouds. It's fantastic!'

Just to be polite, I stood up, extended my arm for Ngân to take it, to pull me and tug me back and forth... Nothing stood out to me except the fact that our shoes kept touching each other, the entire ordeal kind of ludicrous, comical, and... just strange. I gave up after some awkward dancing, so Ngân let me go, her body doubled over from laughing. As another melody started playing and one of the girls took a break, the 'dance professor' mocked Ngân for her disservice to ballroom dancing, then turned to extend his hand to me, gentle and gracious.

'My dear lady, Ngân is only a student of mine, so she's in no position to teach anyone! If my dear lady would follow me, I shall *entraîner* you for ten minutes, and the high art of ballroom dancing will all become clear to you.'

Given the situation and the space we were in, I felt it might not be polite to reject him. Before I could make up my mind, the young man had already pulled on my arm with one hand, his other arm holding my back. He lifted his face toward the ceiling, solemn like a believer tuning into God's song. Chasing after the rhythm of the trumpet, he shoved his right thigh in between my... crotch. My cheeks flushed in embarrassment, a peculiar electric current coursing through me as my mind became muddled and my soul flew out of my body! I was at the mercy of this guide's smooth moves, all while trying to monitor my movements to avoid colliding knees or toe caps... I'd managed to suppress with all my might that bodily buzz in the peak of puberty, yet it abruptly erupted with singular force. That sensation was not yet pleasure, but more intense than lust. It toyed with the boundary of truth and jest. It grew stronger, unrelenting, one rush of heat unquelled rolling right into another new rush. It held us from release, forcing unending floods of desire to gush out... I had to put my head on the guide's shoulders, fearful that my face would give my feelings away at once. I was frightened that they might find out how mortified I felt.

And thus this Huyền kept on brazenly chasing those feelings, because that was art, because everyone around Huyền was doing the same. It was a lust with power, a lust acknowledged and encouraged, a lust for the civilised! It wasn't considered illegitimate lust, even though it was just another embodiment of illegitimate lust. It was protected by both the arts and the law. All the while, Ngân was observing us with eyes of adoration and ambition!

I would've remained blissful just like that until the end of time—until my guide's hand clutched mine with a grip that terrified me, his arm wrapped impossibly tight around my back, his lips quivered as if begging for a kiss, his eyes glazed over as if his soul had left his body, a sign of reaching climax... Even the guide noticed his emotional crisis, the rhythm of the trumpet lost, his steps crisscrossing, stumbling... I shivered. My body froze. He immediately let go of me, took a seat, panting and trying to save face.

'What a waste! We were killing it and my dear lady just stopped! You have a knack for dancing, though. Those sweet moves... you must've practised a few yourself.'

I snapped back.

'No, I haven't practised anything!'

I sat down next to Ngân. The professor complimented me again.

'A handful of lessons and you'll be a virtuoso.'

My face flushed for obvious reasons. I wished Ngân would chime in and save me from the embarrassment, but as the music changed to a different record, she had already stood up and asked the professor to wrap up the valse they'd been learning.

That day marked the return of debilitating sensations. The trial dance rekindled my dirty thoughts and carnal desires which had once dissolved like charcoal burning away in the ashy breeze. Now, they were blowing up like a whirlwind of dry sawdust. Oh, how joyous now that even filthy fantasies were protected by creative interpretations that exacerbated their pollution of man's nature. My licentious thoughts were no longer dirty, but in fact justified—for whenever I closed my eyes, I only dreamed of sinking myself into my ideal man's embrace—Nguyễn Lưu's. With the sudden and mighty awakening of my logical mind, my love for Nguyễn Lưu was no longer an idea in my head. That man was already my husband, which meant all bets were off, and thus my lewd fantasies of him were certainly not illegitimate lust.

You could say I was a product of my environment.

But if that were the sole cause, I wouldn't have turned out this way...

The next morning, my father and his mistress made merry downtown while Lưu and my oldest brother went to the cinema. Alone in the spacious attic, I wanted to replicate a new shirt design and, in my search for a pencil, rummaged through my rogue brother's backpack. As soon as I pulled out the books weighing down the overloaded bag, a pile of photos spattered out, scattering everywhere in front of me... What kind of photos? There were five of them, two of which were prints of two nude Western beauties, while the others were... they were... The stillness of the house encouraged my curiosity. I studied them with as much enthusiasm as any other woman would've done... My heart was pounding so hard as though it was leaping out of my chest, all of my five senses alert as though roused by a dose of premium tonics, my mind in paralysing awe... I examined those terrific photos for hours, unable to tear my eyes off them, my hands moving on their own.

No matter the catastrophe, we can still find an innate goodness in the human heart. That is to say, my conscience found its way back to me. I came to find myself filthy and despicable. With utmost determination, I gathered the photos, slotted them back in the book and into the backpack, folded it, then went to sit in the backyard. I'd managed to wipe out that haunting force! Dear me! Who would've thought that was the extent of my brother's studies? I went to bed with a whirlwind of thoughts in my mind and buried myself under the blanket like I was sick... Still, those photos followed me under the fleece blanket. I closed my eyes, but alas, the Creator cruelly gifted us this strange ability to see even with our eyes closed. My eyelids became a projector that replayed those three obscene photos over and over again! I slid my fingers into my mouth, bit down on them as if they were my enemy's. The pangs of pain weren't enough to chase off those lustful thoughts. At my wit's end, I planted my face on my pillow, blocking both my nose and mouth, holding my breath until my chest ached, almost like a victim of suicide. I kept at it for a long... long time, before I exhausted myself and drifted off to oblivion.

I didn't know when I fell asleep, but it was tumultuous, plagued with terrifying dreams.

When I jolted awake, the clock just chimed three in the morning.

I was still upset over my arm, numb as if pricked and crushed by thousands of needles. Behind the green-painted wooden wall where my father and his mistress slept, they began the intimidating acts of love. Smacking kisses, heavy panting, spring bed violently shaking, shrieks of pleasure stirred up the whole room. I sighed silently, then tiptoed off my bed, slid into my coconut slippers, and, like a thief, felt my way down the stairs...

Through the courtyard, I entered my brother's study room and pulled a chair to the window. In the room there was a blackboard and a cane bench. During the day, my brother and his friends would gather here, but at night, he'd leave it empty for mice to take over. I looked up at the moon peeking through the window frame, and realised for the first time the black streaks on the moon's body looking like a banyan tree. The sky, dense with stars, was entrancing; that haunting force gave way to my fascination with this boundless and bottomless universe. My thoughts wandered on and on. When I tired myself out, I didn't even think of going to bed.

I heard someone descending from upstairs. They entered the room... It was Lưu!

He walked past me and stopped for a moment—seemingly out of surprise—then headed straight to the backyard, maybe in need of something. Overcome with shame, I wondered if Lưu, also intimidated by that display of love, was taking refuge. If that was the case, then I'd really wish for a hole to hide in right now. How could my father act like that? Did Lưu see something? Or did he not?

Here... Then... Lưu was making his way back. He took a few steps past me then halted midway. I turned around. After a long silence, he asked,

'Is that you, Huyền?'

'Yes.'

'What... What are you doing, sitting over there?'

'I can't sleep.'

'Me neither. I kept tossing and turning, all for naught.'

Darn it! If that was true, then of course Lưu had noticed that show of irresponsibility of Vietnamese families. But before my shame sunk in, Lưu came close, his voice quiet.

'I just watched a really touching film earlier tonight.'

We'd been avoiding each other for so long that now every word from him frightened me to the core. I feared facing him, even more so his words, because anything he uttered would inflame a longing—a yearning—in my heart. This time, seeing that Lưu had initiated the conversation, I kept my mouth shut, only to hear my heart thumping loudly in my chest. Perhaps to shake off my indifference, Lưu crossed his arms in front of his chest, walked towards me, leaned against the wall, and fixed an imposing gaze on me. Petrified, I only blurted out,

'Is that so!'

'Yes.' With that curt answer, Lưu gripped the chair rail with both hands, and his eyes bored into me. 'It was a love story. A great, terrific tragedy. An intimacy so passionate it posed a horror akin to hatred and resentment. Every imaginable expression of blood thirst, of pleasure, and of death...'

After that ornate monologue, Lưu fell into deep contemplation, seemingly awaiting my judgement. I had no clue what he was talking about, but chimed in anyway:

'Is it that good? How does the story go?'

'A man falls in love with a woman... They love each other dearly, yet can't spend the rest of their lives together... And then... Guess how that story ends?'

'Beats me!'

'The man kills the woman, and then himself! They both die! The man wants to take his own life at first, but fears that another man will snatch away his lover! So he kills her to free his worry, then kills himself! A fascinating story, wouldn't you say?'

'If it's a made-up story then I can probably see the appeal...'

'You think the writer pulled that out of nowhere? No, history documented it.'

'Well, I find that too cruel, too brutal. How could you kill someone you love like that? Come hell or high water, I can never bring myself to kill the person I love.'

Lưu let out a hollow laugh.

'It seems that you haven't been in love. If you love someone, and I mean with obsession, with yearning, with resentment, with honesty, with everything that you have, then you can certainly take that person's life. For example, if I had the fortune to be loved by Huyền like that, to be killed by you like that before you committed suicide, then I would've died with the happiness of every remaining soul in this world!... Or if I could kill Huyền before killing myself... then... that would also be happiness, unless we get to live under one roof.'

Those words, uttered in such an earnest voice of deeply buried grief, gave me chills. Overwhelmed, I stood up reflexively, as if trying to flee. Lưu took his chance and grabbed both of my hands. He sobbed.

'Huyền, oh Huyền! Do you pity me at all, Huyền? I wouldn't go so far as to dream that you would love me as much as I love you, but I thought I at least had the right to hope that you would spare me even a sliver of your affection. Oh lord, you... you can't possibly understand my sorrow. Lưu loves Huyền, so much, so, so much, that I had to say it out loud. I have sewn my mouth shut for the past months, waiting for your response! And yet for the past month, we've been avoiding each other like the plague, and you don't even care to tell me how I should plan my life onward. And now, I just can't stand it any more! Huyền!'

I lowered my head and mumbled,

'But what can I do?'

Lưu answered hurriedly,

'Let's elope! There's no other way! If you love me... if you would sacrifice everything, then we... Would you take that risk with me, and be with me through thick and thin?'

Without hearing my answer, Lưu raised both of my hands to his lips and kissed them. Then slowly, he led me to the bench and forced me into the seat next to him. No words came to my mind. I just sat there, dazed. In moments like this, your wits just vanish into thin air, yielding control to the soul governed by feelings. Lưu's words echoed in my ears ceaselessly, without understanding any of it.

'Huyền, let's brave the world... love will be our reward, happiness our telos... I'll take care of everything... to love Huyền, for the rest of my life... Forever! 'Til death do us part!'

Gently, Lưu wrapped his arms around me, pulling me into a tight embrace. Then, like a madman, he showered me with kisses on the forehead, eyelids, nose, cheeks, chin, neck, then my lips... for a long, long time. A deluge of intimacy and caresses. When I opened my eyes, under the moonlight, Lưu's face had this unusual expression of determination and infatuation. His jaws were puffed up, the skin on his temples slick and tense, and a singular vein was popping on his forehead, wrinkled with courage.

Silky silence surrounded us, the room as quiet as a graveyard.

I felt as if the universe were in my hands—or at least I'd completely forgotten that the universe existed around me. My worries evaporated. There was nothing but joy in my heart, for Lưu was clearly in love with me... My husband! My doting, pampering husband whom I could only find in my dreams!

...I could hardly recall any of Lưu's loving whispers. He had claimed me, body and soul.

And the inevitable happened.

The morning after, as I recovered from my fatigue, reality dawned on me. Did I dream of it? No, I had tasted life through something real. My injured, torn flesh still ached. Only now did I come to understand fully the terror of unmarried girls who took a risky bet on love. I had been deflowered! Fear, confusion, pain, concern, shame, and self-denial cycled through me—like every other girl who had lost their virginity. But it was too late. Because the Creator didn't make us to reproach ourselves—those who couldn't forgive their own mistakes had taken their own lives already—I had other ideas. The final ideal! Elope! With Lưu, against the world!

Lưu's attitude in the following week somehow reverted to how it was a few months prior, which I thought was frustrating and bizarre. I was looking for a chance to give him a piece of my mind, then came that afternoon...

'No, you aren't getting it. After what happened, I've been reflecting deeply on my mistake. I've been trying to find ways to make amends. There's only one option for us: running away. But where? I'm still a student. You don't have a job to rely on. So, I sent two S.O.S. letters to two of my old friends in the South, asking them to find us jobs or prepare shelter for us. Then we'll pay them back later, as long as this life away from home doesn't get too bad that we end up jobless.'

Anxiously, I asked,

'What if they can't help us?'

'Huyền, don't tempt fate. I'm certain those people care for me dearly... And if they don't help us for one reason or another, then we'll help ourselves! A small risk is all it takes! Even though my parents aren't rich, if I have to resort to lying to them, I can at least borrow some funds to make a living... Besides, it's not like it's an emergency... We're preparing ahead so that no grass grows under our feet, but we're not in a rush, are we?'

Those plans didn't reassure me, because something felt... off! The two of us had already taken the leap and committed that mistake, so couldn't we just find a way to marry each other the official way? At most, the public would judge our marriage for being between distant cousins, but no tradition or law could prohibit us. Lưu's plan would only render our illicit affair even more so!

I said,

'Then why don't you just think of a way to deal with this within the bounds of law? Wouldn't that be better?'

Lưu snapped.

'Oh, you think I haven't tried that? If that were possible, why would I sneak around and torture my soul over it? Yes, we're only distant cousins, so of course, our marriage doesn't violate any moral code. But there's the public: the public with their scathing opinions. Especially when I've already been a tenant in this house and grown so close with you. Even your parents or my parents wouldn't accept us so readily and happily. And you know very well what kind of people they are! If they don't accept us, then there's nothing we can do to win them over! If we cry stinking fish out of nowhere like you said, nothing good will come out of it, and eloping would simply be impossible!'

After a moment of thinking, Lưu continued.

'That's how it is, dear. Our parents could never imagine us messing up this hard—not in their wildest dreams. You think you have the courage to confess? What if our seniors take precautions by isolating us? Besides, I must also protect your reputation with all my might... Our folly must be kept a secret, even from our parents! I think there's only one way, and that's running away. If we try to talk and it doesn't work out, then even our mutual happiness would be torn to shreds!'

'If you've thought it through, then be my guest.'

'Our best bet is to just leave our families, quietly move away, then build our own domestic life. When we mature into proper adults, we'll return and own up to our crime with pride and valour. That'll be when I have a more or less profitable business, and you with two little ones on your hands. No matter how upset our parents may be, they'll have to deal with it. Or else... if we end up pinching pennies, then...'

In that moment, I was filled with joy. Every word Lưu uttered moved me to put my trust in the future, to remain positive... I smiled and picked up where he left off.

'Then we won't meet our parents ever again?'

Lưu shrugged his shoulders.

'Of course! If we don't amount to anything, then we shouldn't come back anyway. That will trouble them even further.'

Then we split up.

My joy lasted for just about a week, when my mother suddenly came back from her hometown... I could still recall that day clearly: I was sewing a scarf when my mother stepped inside the house. For some reason, my heart started pounding as if out of fearful anticipation, but of what I didn't have a clue. It came from the intuition only shared between mother and child... My folly with Lưu meant a betrayal against my mother. Once a child wronged their mother, the heart would quiver to confess, even if the mouth wanted to remain shut! My will didn't matter! Stunned and terrified, I thought my mother had uncovered my crime with just a glance at my face...

That afternoon, I learned that my mother came back home because there was a civil servant named Kim who wanted to wed me. And it seemed like my father had agreed! My mother just needed to handle the dowry! Apparently that Kim had visited our house to assess me, and for father to assess him. I served him drinks myself, but we always had guests over, so I really wasn't sure. This turn of events was too dreadful!

When my mother told me that 'good' news, I pulled out every tactful excuse to reject it, which I need not repeat here. At her wits' end, my mother broke into tears as she tried to talk some sense into me.

'My child, if you love us, then accept him! You're still young and naïve, there's so much you don't know, and now I have to spell it out for you; that I have to spell it out to you troubles me greatly. Don't you know that ever since your father took in that mistress, I've had no standing in this house anymore? If I die while you remain unwed, then you're just going to suffer for the rest of your life! Now, I'm still here and a man of prestige has asked for your hand. Yet you're not happy with this golden ticket— you don't want to break free from this misery. How can I die with my eyes closed if you keep this up? Your father has made my life hell already, so take some pity on me, will you? Who knows when I'll bite the dust? I'm on pins and needles just thinking about your younger siblings living with their stepmum!'

I didn't know what else to say. When your own mother uses tears to sway you, what kind of child would dare disagree? The evening after was my father's turn to threaten me. An evening of tragedy that I can never forget.

'Why do you want to turn him down, my child?'

'Dear father, I do not understand the reason myself. But something feels peculiar to me! I feel like if I become that person's wife, I will suffer. I do not understand why I cannot bring myself to approve of that person, either, even though he is a very worthy man of formidable prestige... Perhaps fate does not allow it.'

My father, still gentle, explained,

'Just think about it! A handsome young man, an only child with well-off parents, a meticulous *administrateur*. He's got the prestige, the rank, the looks. That's the best any girl could hope for! You should get off your high horse now. It'd be mortifying if you end up with someone lesser.'

'Dear father, if you could give me more time to think

about it…'

He laughed hollowly.

'I've already agreed! You don't have to think about anything. You'll get married in ten days. You have me to take care of this, and that's enough. I'm not so dim-witted as to refuse to recognise that I might be forcing you, and that man isn't so spineless that he'd tell me to force you.'

For some reason, I felt bold enough to snap back.

'That is my entire future. You should have let me decide…'

As soon as I uttered those words, my father banged his fist down on the table. A shadow cast over my face; the flower vase and cups felt like they'd fallen off the table and shattered into pieces. His eyes blew open and glared with monstrous hostility; he crossed his arms in front of his chest and questioned me.

'Then what good reason do you have to turn down that proposal? Huh? Do you have any good reason? Or did you fall in love with some guy? Did you? Speak. Tell me the truth right now. I'll handle it. I'll have you chase after his ghost…'

Without a single moment to think, I blurted out some nonsense.

'Why on earth would I fall for any guy!'

My father shrugged, cross and content at the same time. He was certain that a person like me wouldn't just fall in love with a guy out of nowhere...

'Then shut up! I'm your father. I have every right to marry you off. You sit wherever I tell you to!'

I had no choice but to shut up. He was right; if I didn't have a good reason, I couldn't make my case. And even if I wanted to take advantage of this situation to confess my crime, I wouldn't dare to, for Lưu had told me to keep quiet!

From then, my parents didn't feel the need to further console or counsel me. They just let things unfold as planned.

Two days later, when the house was vacant, Lưu spoke under his breath.

'I urge Huyền to rest assured. Although out of the two letters I sent, one's returned bearing disappointing news, you just need to believe in me. There are still two more weeks, so I hope you'll allow me a couple more days and not fret about a thing.'

As worried as I was, I still had to deceive myself, trying to ease my mind and trust in Lưu. I had no idea that Lưu kept telling me over and over again to keep my composure because he'd already lost it himself. For several days straight, Lưu neither dined nor slept at home... I couldn't keep my anxiety at bay...

And then... that day, at six in the morning, a Western secret agent pounded on our door and asked for my father. He then took him to a brothel as a witness for the coroner, who was examining a suicide case that left a letter addressed to my father! I panicked. The night before, my older brother, dragged out by his friends for an evening out, hadn't come home for the entire night. Hearing the terrible news, my parents' face went pale, terrified that the unlucky person had been their own child. Meanwhile, I suspected that the person who committed suicide was Lưu. The more I thought about it, the harder I prayed to the Heavens and Buddha that it wasn't Lưu. Not that I wasn't worried about my brother—but no matter how much I tried to expel them, all my doubts went straight to Lưu's fate.

Indeed, Nguyễn Lưu had taken his own life! I followed my father into the brothel room where they said the misfortune occurred. And there I saw him, strewn across the attic floor, his head leaning a bit backward, black foam fizzing out of his mouth, his eyes half-closed and bloodshot. That poor bastard was no other than Nguyễn Lưu: my lover. My mind went haywire, my limbs weak, barely holding myself up... Yet strangely, out of nowhere, an invisible power calmed me down. In that moment of imminent danger, I was dead set that despite Lưu's death, this Huyền would never let anyone expose our affair. Huyền would protect the integrity of Lưu's reputation. And future Huyền would handle anything that came her way...

The coroner performed a preliminary examination on Lưu's corpse, then told my father that Lưu killed himself with opium. The agent also made a report, and my father took care of Lưu's burial. Lưu was dead. The letter Lưu left was only an apology to my father and some rambling about how he'd grown sick of life and wanted to die. Lưu never mentioned anything about me and him. Out of agony, I came home and rummaged through my drawer and books and notes to see if Lưu left any notes for me, but it was all in vain.

The suicide happened three days before my wedding and my entire household was thrown into chaos. But I wasn't affected in the slightest. No one dared mention it after Lưu's burial, as a joyous event was soon occurring. Lưu's parents came to manage his funeral but didn't have the face to frequent my place too much, either.

As for me, that pain drove me to use my corruptness to seek revenge against my parents and bring shame upon my soon-to-be husband. Because everyone was responsible for Lửu's death, I'd make everyone suffer and fall apart; I'd disgrace and humiliate them. Deflowered! That meant the pig on the second day of my wedding ceremony would have its earlobes cut off! That would humiliate my parents horribly! How lucky I was to have been deflowered, because what other method of revenge could be more malevolent? Yes, revenge, and revenge!

And as for my life... well, I'd know what to do when the time came.

III - Married Life

The groom's family directed this marriage with the speed of an express train. A deluge of rushed notices and letters, marriage gifts, the engagement ceremony, and the wedding itself—all in two weeks! It wasn't because they were afraid that the longer the wait, the greater the heart wandered. In the groom's extended family, there was an old lady who was on her deathbed, and no one could tell when she'd kick the bucket, so they wanted to get the wedding done as soon as humanly possible. Everything wrapped up so quickly that I had no time to reconsider my valiant and meaningless idea to avenge Lưu with a smear campaign against my and my husband's families: the ones I blamed for Lưu's death despite their innocence—yes, that brave and bold idea. In a situation such as mine, an impulsive decision was as set in stone as a plan that left no stone unturned. In those short two weeks, I spent every waking hour greeting guests and handling preparations. My heart still in pieces over my lover's suicide, I couldn't care less about my relatives' good wishes and my friends' jokes—even the ones closest to me. Every word seemed so redundant, insignificant, and unworthy of my attention. One day I'd clean the house for painters to plaster lime, the next day I'd get groceries for the feast, then the day after that I'd go pick out clothes. One morning was for the tailor, another evening for the goldsmith, then the next day for printing wedding invitations. Whenever I took a break, my friends and sisters would come to pester me right then and there. They said they'd come 'help', but they only added more chaos to the mix. A daily routine of pure tedium was enough mockery to train my expression into collected indifference, so much so that everyone must've thought I was content with the marriage, my heart entirely devoid of tragedy. I didn't even fear the calamitous mess waiting for me: a already deflowered yet unwed girl.

Having made up my mind to commit suicide, I desired nothing but the pain of my most beloved people. The suicidal, without regard for their reputation, only wanted revenge by inflicting pain on others. And to me, bringing my unwhole body to my husband's home was just another method of suicide.

On the day of the wedding, I stepped into a limousine

adorned with flower bouquets. As we passed through the rope of fate, among constantly giggling flower girls dressed in flashy clothes, I moved like a machine, not a flicker of shame or confusion. I seemed to have assumed the precarious fate of a man-eater, this marriage not my first, and, having exhausted myself from incessant scepticism toward happiness, I felt neither self-consciousness nor contentment, only wariness and, thus, repose...

Complicated rituals concluded, I was led into the bride's chamber. A clean, fragrant room painted in playful colours, with a faint scent of freshly washed blankets and pillows. Standing in front of these brand-new pieces of furniture reminded me that I was a 'used' bride. I suddenly quivered with fear. I regretted my audacity going into this marriage. Why didn't I reject it right away? Or perhaps I could've delayed it to find a way out. And if that didn't work out, I should've simply run away, even though I had no clue where... I didn't realise how insane I was until now—and now it was too late. The reasons I once came up with to defend my revenge had now vanished from my lonesome mind. Regardless of what had happened, my husband hadn't done anything wrong to deserve my 'revenge'. Regardless of what had happened, my parents didn't deserve to have their names dragged through the mud... Deflowered! A deflowered girl shouldn't get married to begin with! Being deflowered didn't give you the right to drive your parents to shame, your husband to drastic measures, and yourself to more shame and folly!

Then what to do next?

Long ago, when I was still in school, a girl told me that if a young lady had accidentally done the deed, a certain chemical mixture could recover the wholeness of her maidenhood to serve to her esteemed husband on the wedding night. I wasn't listening, though, so I couldn't recall any of those magical chemical elements, and even if I did, there was no time! Besides, I believed some Western doctor said the paper-thin hymen, on which a girl staked her honour as a woman, could tear from a hard fall or a slip of the foot. There were also women who didn't have a maidenhood even without intercourse, because the Creator didn't give her one to begin with...

Having recalled those things, I found my husband a lot easier to deal with. If I could keep my quick wits about me and handle this delicately, I doubted my husband could tell of my corruption. As a woman's honour fundamentally depended on an object as minute and vulnerable as the hymen, her small gestures—such as a shy and innocent expression, or a subtle, tight hip squeeze to impede and pain the groom—could save the woman as well! If the bridegroom found nothing suspicious, then surely he wouldn't notice the existence or lack thereof of a few drops of blood on bản paper. During consummation, I'd prohibit my groom from turning on the lights. As for the blood... one could easily obtain some with a sharp knife tip or pin from a turban... O! The game of life and the heart of man! If my scheme led me to great victory, then despicable I'd be, but still... have a look at *why* I became despicable.

Then again, what if I performed the most innocent gestures and words known to mankind, and my husband still picked me apart? I'd probably have to put on an astounded front, feigning ignorance to everything! An *administrateur* himself, my husband surely would've received the education to come to his own conclusion whether he wished to avoid pain and deceive himself. A woman's maidenhood was a highly complex issue that even science didn't have all the answers to yet! If push came to shove, I'd cling onto the man's intellectual capacity—that is, his ego, so that he would become just as sceptical as scientists if he got his hands on a book on that topic.

And if all else failed, then I'd fight back with all I had! Facing his outraged interrogation, I wouldn't talk back with haste, but rather let my bridegroom criticise me to his heart's content, and I'd leisurely say something along these lines:

'Yes sir, yes! Before I came here, I was already another man's wife! Do not blame me, but rather yourself! Surely you already know this: in the midst of this transitional period, how intense the conflict between old and new can be, as well as the great tragedy of our time! Surely you already know that most women in the nation want to choose their own partner for life, while their parents only want to force their decisions on them. A young and progressive man like you must understand this, don't you? And yet you're behaving like a caveman. You didn't give two hoots whether the person you wished to marry wanted to happily come with you? Moreover, you already took advantage of your reputation and rank to violate the lives of two other people on this earth! Dear sir, you think you're a good man, but you're actually evil without even knowing it. There could've been a couple who was about to enjoy the delight of family life, and then you had to come with your position as an *administrateur* and your several houses to completely demolish their happiness!'

I'd say all that, without batting an eye.

No! I wouldn't stop at just that; I'd keep on talking!

'A young man resorted to suicide because of you, good sir! In front of you right now is his accursed widow, the wife of that man who killed himself: a woman who could no longer preserve her loyalty for her dead spouse, for you have forced yourself onto me. You have even done it within the bounds of the law, and yet you scorn me for not being a virgin any more, sir! I rest my case. You take it however you want...'

Yes, exactly! I shall say it nonchalantly yet firmly, elegantly yet unyieldingly, thereby absolving my crime while condemning my bridegroom so that he felt guilty on his own, in spite of the fact that his new wife had already been deflowered! And what was to come, I'd deal with it then...

And what was to come... if the pig had its ears cut off, if the groom came to berate the wife's parents, if the bride was sent back to her own home, then I would've avenged Lưu. Certainly! Fantastic—just watch the havoc I'd wreak! Even though Lưu had already died, just watch me announce to the entire world that Lưu was already my husband! Honour or humiliation—both are simply meaningless nouns blabbered out from the mouths of the unthinking.

With extreme concentration, I revised over and over again the words that, if pushed to the point of no return, I'd recite out loud. These words were seemingly a form of literature themselves. Just like that, my novel-influenced mind had imagined a blasphemous act into such a poetic act.

For several hours, I kept on sitting, lost in thought, next to a red silk blanket and two phoenix-embroidered pillows, in front of a housemaid who was dozing off. Every once in a while, my bridegroom would drop by the room to put something away or to look for something in a cabinet. One time, he struck up a conversation with a smile, asking, 'Is my wife homesick already?', but I only bowed my head in silence...

He was an average-sized man, not handsome but not ugly, not fat but not skinny, his face naïve like that of every other person born with a silver spoon in their mouth. It was a nonsensical face; whenever you looked at it, you wouldn't be able to feel even a shred of sympathy— or even of antipathy, for that matter! His unremarkable face reminded me of the kind of young man who didn't have the most stellar academic record, with extremely mediocre intellect and no other ambitious aspirations besides working towards passing his certifications, scoring a position in the government, and marrying a pretty wife. It was likely that he had bribed to pass his classes, bribed to pass his exams, bribed to obtain his position—all in all the kind of person who, without his rich parents, could resort to only bastardly methods... If that man were born into riches and honour, he would only end up a freeloader... No! For that kind of person, happiness would be an impossible feat, and to act cunningly around them would be overdoing it! To deceive a husband of that kind, who didn't know I was deflowered, I'd be better off looking down on him. Even if he forgave me, I'd just find him even more contemptuous! It seemed as if Lưu's vengeful spirit was still lurking somewhere around here.

The afternoon had entered the twilight zone... A sombre darkness suddenly invaded the entire room. Lights throughout the house were turned on one by one, but they brought no ray of light to my heart. Only a few hours left... My entire being felt numb, as if my soul as if had almost completely dissolved somewhere else, while the body that remained was like a sluggish, paralysed lump of meat; I thought a person who was sentenced to death before the guillotine would feel as anxious and conflicted as I was, counting every second! Consummation! That noun would've been beautiful, if my bridegroom were Nguyễn Lưu! And yet that noun had now become so tasteless that it couldn't invoke in me a single sliver of fleshly desire, even though that pleasure should've been the climax, the most satisfying out of all kinds of pleasure.

'Pour me two glasses of water, then go downstairs and see if the elderly want anything.'

The housemaid obeyed. My bridegroom took off the scarf still fixed on his head and the blue brocade robe, leaving on only a long white shirt. After the housemaid was completely out of sight, he quietly closed the door then came to sit next to me and held my hands... Seeing me shyly lower my head, he tenderly lifted my hands to his lips and gently placed a kiss on my knuckles. Then, my husband, still holding my hands, stood up and led me to the chair and the small table about two metres away from the bed.

'Have a seat here, so that we, husband and wife, can have a chat first! Now, will you have some water?'

As soon as he finished his sentence, he raised the glass to my mouth with one hand, and placing the other hand on my chin, as if he saw me as an infant who couldn't yet drink a glass of water without making a mess. Such a gesture would've been so intimate, so earnest, so touching, if not for the word 'first' that he just accidentally uttered... Just that one word was enough to annihilate the suaveness and sincerity in that gesture, to make me feel all the acidity of the wedding ceremonies, the irony of marriage, and endlessly so the cruelty of the human heart. My husband's passionate invitation only backfired, rendering my impression of him even more adverse. At that moment, I wanted my bridegroom to stop acting so endearingly: every act of endearment was merely another act of mockery in disguise... I was further convinced that my bridegroom was, if not a mediocre man, then a fool. Because a fool was usually well-versed in the art of seducing women. 'No! I beg you not to utter such words and bring out such gestures. I'm losing my mind over here! Would you please come a little closer, be a little cruder, and stop sucking up to me. If you're a husband, then please talk like a husband—that is, like a king. I want to fear you a little, to admit to my mistakes a little, to regret a lot, so that later on I can come to love you, because now I've already... lost my virginity!' I wanted to say all that, right then and there.

Seeing my lowered head, my beet-red cheeks, my bridegroom seemed to assume it was the innocence, the purity, the flustering of a young woman's first intimate interaction with a man. He became ten times more infatuated.

'Huyền, oh Huyền! What are you thinking in moments like this? What do you think about me? Could I be a deserving husband to you? Huyền?'

And so my bridegroom kept on blabbering to himself, as I tried my best to put on various innocent gestures by lowering my face then pulling my shirt hem to my mouth... The me in front of my bridegroom was an untouched girl: pure, shy, ignorant. Those were the conditions required to grant total happiness to every bridegroom.

He told me that he 'had had a crush' on me only

after a few times of meeting me, yet he didn't have the opportunity to convey his feelings. He'd been holding in the agony of harbouring a love in secret. Now that he had married me, he was immensely satisfied; in fact, he couldn't have even imagined it, couldn't have expected this happiness to come to him so easily and so quickly. Yet, there was one thing that he felt dissatisfied about— that is, the fact that we didn't marry on the basis of love. Should we have known each other from before and fallen crazily in love with each other, then our marriage would've been tremendously more romantic. But that problem wasn't entirely hopeless, if I came to love him. Not the type of love like in the law, but the special type of love basked in a lover's diverse feelings of resentment, nagging, despondence, and hatred. My bridegroom said that even though we were already husband and wife, he still maintained his position and loved me as a suitor, and wanted me to reciprocate.

'Huyền, I desperately wish that we could forgo our duties in this matter. If I love Huyền, or Huyền loves me, just out of duty, then doesn't that mean there's no love between the two of us? What are duties, then, if not obligations? And if love is based on obligations, then what value does it have? Love is an incredibly precious feeling, one that we can't beg for or threaten out of someone, and even if the law, morals, ethics, and tradition form an alliance to chain down love, that wouldn't work, either. So I need you to allow me to indulge in a love that comes from the sincerity of your heart.'

Ah! I see that the man I deemed foolish and mediocre just earlier had now suddenly reformed himself before my eyes. There was no way a man who knew nothing about anything could express himself with such clarity. This man is a man with experience! That blade-like tongue of his must've murmured into the ears of many different types of women his philosophical takes on love or intoxicating sweet nothings. Even the streetwalkers, with their seasoned and jaded steel souls, would likely be moved to ruin if met with this type of rhetoric...

And, after all, those words of love would only result in an unfavourable outcome—that is, planting a horrific sense of dread in my heart.

I must take extreme caution.

Facing those attentive eyes gazing up at me boiling with anticipation for my answer, I lowered my head again and muttered,

'I understand.'

With a content look on his face, my bridegroom inched his chair closer to me, took the round silk pillow and slotted it behind my back, wrapped his two hands around me in a tight embrace, and fixed his glare on me as if watching a masterpiece depicting a great beauty. Then, he kissed me right on the lips like in the movies. My heart pounded; my entire body suddenly limp. After the kiss, my bridegroom remained leaning forward, resting on my chest, yearning to watch me for an eternity, but then I shyly pushed him away, as the hem of my headscarf was about to come loose... Once I sat up straight, from then on, I only had to respond to my husband's questions about my family, my education, my friends, and other trivial, tangential concerns.

Time was flying by, and the bell chimed nine before we knew it.

'That's all. Go get comfortably dressed now; today... must've been exhausting. There'll be more annoying things on the second day of the ceremony to deal with, so let's rest.'

That night, after his terrifying act of seduction, I didn't see my bridegroom come in to check for some cotton towel or some pile of bản paper like most bridegrooms. He went to bed before me, and into a deep slumber he fell.

My anxious conflict had been prolonged until the following evening. It seemed as if no thoughts of suspicion had crossed my bridegroom's mind. His unceasing hugs, his gentle touches, his shower of kisses—they were filled with a genuine affection and respect for his wife. A husband who knew that his wife had not been unmarked would never have been able to put up such a passionate pretence.

And let Huyền tell you right now, that kind of half-hearted, wishy-washy consummation went on for the entire six, seven nights!

As I lay next to a player husband who'd pulled all sorts of weird tricks on me—in moments where my flesh trembled, my senses awakened to welcome the ultimate climax—my husband would take both of my hands off, turn his back to me and go to sleep. Sometimes, when I woke in the middle of the night and glanced to my side, my husband had already left our bed and returned to his private room. What a shock—how life turned out like this! What a punishment if our honeymoon came down to this! Why was it like this? I couldn't figure it out for the life of me. I was unable to decide on how to handle this, for my husband's sudden change threw all of my plans into turmoil. Many times I had to revise and recite my counterarguments in anticipation of the final event, so that I could firmly assert my viewpoint and my one and only resolution. Yet, as soon as we were close to that final destination of lovemaking, my husband flipped everything on its head and forced me to continue holding on to my secret. Those first seven nights were nothing but incessant stimulations and frustrating ambiguity. Everything had been turned upside down. It was time for me not to fear being interrogated by my esteemed husband any more, but rather for me to interrogate that esteemed husband!

Life turned out to be anything but my far-flung anxieties. If you were worried for me, a girl deflowered before her marriage, you'd be in for a great surprise. That is to say, I should've been denying or disgracefully confessing my sin to my husband, but in contrast, it was my husband who confessed his sin to me! My almost-a-judge husband suddenly became the offender... Such an extraordinary reversal of roles turned out to take root in very mundane aspects of life: my husband was afflicted with syphilis!

'It's not a big deal. I'll recover in no time. We'll be able to share the same bed as true husband and wife in no time. You rest assured. I'm still being treated for it, so I'm probably fine now, but I'm abstaining this much just in case. Don't tell your parents about this, or we'll never hear the end of it.'

When I reacted all sulky, disgusted, and hurt, my husband consoled me.

'Oh, won't you stop being like that? I told you it's not

a big deal! It's nothing out of the ordinary for men these days to be infected with sexually transmitted diseases! There are plenty of young people who have it out there. They even get it several times in a row. I just so happen to be unlucky enough to contract this for the first time. Men like me are already super well-behaved, alright?'

And from that point on, I gained an all-encompassing power, a divine and sacrosanct right—that is, the right to chase my husband off the bed as my territory, like warding off a disgusting, repulsive leper...

It was a grace period I could extend to eternity so that I could recover my virginity! To expand my rights even further, I interrogated my husband about his medications and treatment like a jealous wife, and seeing that he wasn't taking Western medications, I immediately thought of my uncle...

I assured my husband that we were only paying my uncle a visit. Never would he imagine that in the midst of our cordial conversation, I'd suddenly expose my husband's disease to my uncle. As soon as he heard it, my doctor uncle's eyes blew wide open; he sprung right up.

'What the hell! How could that be? You've only been married for just a handful of days!'

Bitterly I responded right away.

'Dear uncle, my husband already had it several months before marrying me.'

Then I reciprocated my husband's glares with even more disdainful and angry glares. Flustered red, my husband stammered.

'But... Dear uncle, I'm close to a complete recovery now.'

My doctor uncle shook and complained.

'If you're not careful, you'll infect your wife with it too!'

I immediately took my chance and said.

'Please have a look at my husband... He's only taking traditional medicine, so I can't be certain he's going to recover!'

In the blink of an eye, the doctor commanded that the patient move to the room next door! About half an hour later, both of them came out, the doctor with a victorious look on his face while my husband wore a fearful expression. Then my uncle said,

'No need for a blood test. Looking at that fading red ring around the skin, it's clear that the disease has progressed to the second phase... Don't think that means you're recovering. You must cure it immediately; if not, once it enters the third phase, you're done for. Many would think they're cured, but in fact, the bacterium is penetrating deep inside you, into the bone and marrow, and so it shows no external symptoms. But once it does, it's over: you're a goner. Some people just drop dead while carrying on with their day, which can seem like a cold, but it's actually because the syphilis bacterium has infiltrated the brain. This is an extremely dangerous disease, and can spread to three generations below if you don't apply definitive treatment. The complications are the true horror here, especially if you happen to contract a different illness later on, which will give the syphilis bacterium the opportunity to wreak havoc over your entire body. By then, it'll be extremely difficult for doctors to treat both at the same time.'

As quickly as scientists who fear suspicion, my uncle briskly reached for his bookshelf and opened a book in front of my husband. Coming over to read, I was horrified when my eyes caught the coloured photos of punctured and pulverised crotches, nauseating and disgusting swelling cysts, and the stunted, chipped, oozing, and slimy genitals, all utterly harrowing!

Yet my husband still asked awkwardly.

'Dear uncle, so that means our traditional medicine won't cure it?'

'Not a chance! I guarantee you, not a chance. We must provide definitive treatment, whereas traditional medicine can only cure the illness as it manifests. Then twenty, thirty years later, the disease will have complications and spread to other organs. People will think that's a different disease, but all in all it's still a part of syphilis.'

'Then if I get Western medications, how long would that take?'

'Two years! Three injections a year. And you have to practice absolute abstinence: no intimacy with your wife, no alcohol, no exotic food. Also wash your clothes separately. You must remember that this disease is highly contagious. If you happen to have an acne, a cyst, or a cut, and you accidentally brush it against the patient's clothes, the bacterium will enter your bloodstream. So think of it as if you're attending a songstress's performance: you're not having intercourse, yet you're already infected. Don't see it as strange. A woman, while brushing her teeth, is already like you; one who accidentally scratched her gum, and when you two kiss on the lips and suck on the tongues, that's enough for the disease to transfer over!'

As my uncle spoke, my husband sat dazed, wracked by terrible anxiety. The doctor continued.

'You should get it treated immediately. If you were a

stranger, it wouldn't matter if you listen to me... But I'm your wife's uncle, so you should listen to me immediately. I'll charge you for the medications only so that both of you can get treated. Since she's my niece I can instruct her to do as she's told. Sweet lord! Why didn't you wait to get married until you were fully cured?'

Hastily, I replied,

'Dear uncle, even though it's turned out like this, my husband is a reasonable man. I haven't contracted the disease yet, because ever since we married, he's been keeping his distance from me...'

My uncle nodded.

'That's very good! But regardless, you should take a blood test. Prevention is better than cure. If your heart and kidneys are fine then we'll give you a 914 injection[1].'

Thus that surprise diagnosis concluded with one injection after another. My happiness was indescribable.

And like that, I now had months, even years to recover my maidenhood. For reasons that were hard to articulate, I couldn't find those precious chemicals for the life of me. As time went on, I didn't think that that task was as significant. My husband still devoted himself to me

---

[1] A popular syphilis treatment at the time.

as promised and cherished me like a lover. His mistake was a justified excuse for me to torment him as I pleased. As Huyền no longer concerned herself with having lost her virginity, time also blurred away Nguyễn Lưu's death in her memory. How absurd! What in the devil was the human heart? Why was I such a miserable mess on the day of Lưu's death, as if I couldn't live another single second on earth, and yet now I was so quick to forget all about him? How infuriating and despicable of me, yet how could I live on without being infuriating and despicable? No matter how desperately I wished and forced myself to miss Lưu, I couldn't. I wanted to writhe in agony, the same agony that I felt when Lưu had just committed suicide so that I could be a human with a conscience. But why could my heart not be bothered? I wanted to dislike my husband, yet I was wavering ever so slightly already... I was feeling something completely in opposition to dislike, something like fondness, if not precisely love. I wanted to despise my husband, yet my husband insistently and wholeheartedly loved me, and that revolting syphilis disease was the reason for my parents' reputation, for my happiness! Whichever way I looked at it, I still couldn't object to this fortunate situation.

From then on, I experienced familial happiness. Born to a wealthy family, the two of us asked to move out once we got married. I escaped the daughter-in-law life that not many could. It was only on the occasional death anniversaries and Lunar New Year that I had to meet my husband's parents. Two young newlyweds residing in a spacious building, with an old nanny and a driver for servants while children were still a question mark, I was living a peaceful, leisurely, joyful life, without having to care for anything, ever. Everyone complimented my good fortune. My husband didn't have to give his income to his parents, so the two of us could spend it on anything we wanted. We were constantly indulging in every hobby of the rich and joining the indulgent bunch who used money like paper. On afternoons with nothing to do, I'd dress up, sit in my private car painted in fake tortoiseshell, so that my acquaintances walking by down the streets would look up and murmur among themselves: 'Look! Administrateur Kim's Madame!' Administrateur Kim— my husband—politely spent his monthly wage on all sorts of entertainment for two young newly-weds: wireless tax, vinyl records, photographic plates, movie tickets, foreign cuisine, supplements, medications, ballroom dancing, *jeu des petits chevaux* matches, markets, kayaking practice. Put it all together, give or take a few, it must've been sixty, seventy silvers wasted. A life of one hundred percent materialism, one hundred percent freedom! Those young boys who once had the nerve to fall for me, should they accidentally come across me now, would feel... ample regret and self-pity, surely. But I, who was pampered and treasured by my husband, would only end up deceiving him! A notice to all husbands! And to lovers, too!

Ever since we evolved into what we are today, there have been philosophers who assert that a woman's heart is incomprehensible, cunning, debased, and untrustworthy. There was even some psychologist who said there was a type of woman who must be tortured in order to behave properly. Women liked it rough rather than gentle, like donkeys. While I knew that those beliefs didn't amount to any definitive law, after contemplation, they might be true in many circumstances. I said so for I was speaking from my own experience...

An outsider, upon seeing a woman with a well-off, devoted husband commit the act of betrayal against him, could only come up with one name to call that woman: a monster. Once the story had arrived at such an end, then there was no reasoning to be had; thus any scientific effort to trace the root cause of this monster, no matter how elaborate, would be in vain. A monster, with its implications of corruption and salacity...

Was that really the truth?

My husband was the optimistic kind, so blindly and thoughtlessly optimistic that, for example, he'd view dancing as an act of politeness. The perpetually changing clothing trends were signs of progress, and he would allow his wife to meet and greet men freely as if expressing his love for his wife like a Westerner. Indeed, my husband would never go so far as to imagine that more dancing meant more sexual provocation; the obsession with chasing after fashion trends meant negligence of other important familial matters; and that a woman let too loose meant instant corruption. No matter what it was, my husband would see only its bright side, but everything in life had its good and bad, its pros and cons.

Moreover, he submitted himself to me. Having been pampered for so long, I suddenly no longer felt compelled to preserve my husband's love like most wives who weren't extremely loved by their husbands. I scorned my husband terribly, for I felt as if he accidentally did something so deplorable that I wouldn't love him any more, he would've fallen into such despair that he'd commit suicide right away. Love, if not within the bounds of mutual respect, would no longer be love. Love, if not within the bounds of desire, would change... Generally speaking, other girls would die to be in my place: a young husband who had money and reputation, and cherished his wife like a Western man, and so on... And yet I, who had all those things in my grasp, found them terribly mundane, and my true happiness lay elsewhere.

Those are some of the principles one could gather from the way I betrayed my husband, something that people considered 'inexplicable'. Other than that, there was also mankind's shameful matter of carnal satisfaction. In any two-timing affair, that problem always plays a significant role, even though it has been disdainfully acknowledged by the materialists and completely rejected by idealists. I could perceive my significant other as everything to me. In our marriage bed, he was no longer everything. I could acknowledge that my significant other satisfied me in all aspects except one: the aspect of my wifehood.

Not only that, my husband was an incredible fool!

His lust was tormented by the poisonous disease; his fleshly excitement was aggravated by the bacteria in his blood and skin. Every single night, my husband would, without fail, try his best to grant me love despite my resistance and objections. I feared his disease, for I was deflowered. And so, even though there should've been an act that enabled us to indulge in true pleasure, we ended up with gestures that only terrorised our spirits further and drove our bodies to even more desire. The lust that should've been extinguished once every night would, in contrast, be stimulated and agitated hundreds of times more! What an abnormal feat against nature— extraordinary, even, if we wanted to say that. I wanted nothing but for my husband to stop with his half-hearted teasing. My husband wouldn't quit it. I wanted to resist with all my might, too. Yet wrapped within my husband's arms, I had no autonomy any more! And so, even though we should've been sleeping together like true husband and wife, we turned out to be playing with each other like a couple of lovers. He was worried that he'd regret harming a girl whom he couldn't take as his for various reasons, all while she was protecting herself in case he had no choice but to betray her, she would still be untouched and able to marry to another husband.

I can still see vividly those scenes in front of my very eyes. The room was tastefully decorated as if to stir up our youthful hearts. The mattress was soft, the blankets warm, the pillows ornately embroidered, and my body was pampered to the point where I imagined even a rose petal would render my back sleeplessly painful! One night it was in this set of pyjamas, the following night a different one, then the lightly Houbigant-perfumed hair; if my husband slipped under my blankets with such cunning charm, how could one have the heart to refuse him...?

Through those very peculiar provocation methods, man unveiled his true form—that is, an animal. Such was human nature in every sense, endowed with all conditions provided by the Creator. From then on, to me, my husband appeared just a little more despicable, though a little more loveable at the same time as well. And all those pretend pleasures drove me to fantasise about other illusions, urged me to make up my mind and deceive my husband. That was to be expected, wasn't it?

Before I betrayed my husband in the arms of another lover, my husband did a terrible thing—a thing that, afterwards, didn't even help him find out that I'd lost my virginity, which gave me even more reason for me to sleep around with men.

After the first two months, I couldn't bear any more of my husband's obscenities. If he kept behaving like this then his injection treatment would go to waste. I decided to sleep separately and disallow that horny demon to lie next to me. This went on for about four, five nights...

Then, one night, I woke up from the depths of my slumber, though not quite sober just yet. Facing my husband's merciless temper, I had to lie as still as some sort of toy, all the way until my husband let me go and I suddenly realised that it was rape—a true case of rape! And what would come after pleasure, if not contraction!

In response to my words of anger and reproach, my husband just lay there, panting as if nearing his deathbed. Eventually, he threw something on the ground and told me through heavy breaths.

'Stop talking now, my ears are falling off. I told you everything is and will be fine. See, just look at that. I used it to prevent the disease from getting to you.'

'It' was a rubber object, as thin as banyan barks that children used to invert and blow with their mouths to kill time. I threw that personal tool away and hastily washed off all traces of that non-consensual lovemaking. I didn't allow my husband to have any piece of evidence to determine whether or not I still had my virginity. Not until well past noon the following morning did my husband manage to wake up—and in shame, too, never mentioning that night ever again.

I was free! I still preserved in its entirety that lifelong honour of every girl, in my marriage! Life wasn't as troublesome as I'd worried. It seemed that after the incident, my husband, undergoing a drastic inner change, stopped finding ways to get intimate with me and instead held off until he fully recovered. This further encouraged my betrayal.

But how did this person become my sweetheart? It was so long ago; I couldn't remember the details clearly. Besides, life lacked no special occasions for a couple to fall in love. And once a couple desired each other, confession was a non-issue. And not to mention myself, a modern woman! Here was a self-proclaimed modern lady with a tact that was even more natural than a man's when she humoured men, never mind if her husband was there or not. Her speech reached a level of liberty where she could happily talk and jest about all sorts of things, whether it concerned marriage or men and women. Even the most timid, lovesick man would feel a surge of confidence to court her and to express his love.

And yet my lover, while timid in a strategic manner, was in no way a coward. The methods which he used to sway me were extremely subtle, to the point that every word and gesture from him felt like an act of politeness and respect towards me. He warmed my heart, moulding it from a feeling of respect to a feeling of affection, and from that affection to an obsessive desire... When he declared his ultimatum, I was so enfeebled that I couldn't utter a single word to deny or resist it. I couldn't at least pull off a bluff to fool people.

My sisters—just imagine a man with a ruddy face, proof of his invigorating vitality, a straight nose, pearly white teeth, a big chest, broad shoulders, in a pink suit of the finest quality, a valuable camera in hand, standing next to a ladybug sedan! He was 'the ideal man' for every romantic girl thirsting for a modern husband, or a respectable lover, wasn't he? Not only that, his cravats, socks, shirts, gloves—or the way he tilted his head to smoke or opened the car door—all these outstandingly polite mannerisms further captivated me. I was never one to be dazzled by superficial glamour and the trivial things that people disdainfully called materialist... And yet right then and there, these mediocre acts of parading himself, when displayed in front of my eyes, took on a spiritual value. I wouldn't have been able to discover it if I hadn't been able to get close to him physically. He was subtly charismatic, as one would have it.

At this point, self-criticism was perhaps impossible to Huyền. I didn't remember quite enough to try to analyse the extent to which my soul wavered. I already considered the fact that I deceived my husband as a stumble, a slip of a foot, or an insignificant accident to which I gave no further consideration as time went on. I didn't feel any frustration or regret, either.

Once a person tripped for the first time—once a person sacrificed their maidenly diffidence for love when they were still innocent, they wouldn't be able to tell when they started to spiral continuously. Well! It turned out I was no longer pure, after Nguyễn Lưu... that is, before I married! Concerns regarding my diffidence were gone from my conscience, and thus after allowing that man the right to possess my body, I'd never in a million years feel torn and guilty towards my husband. The one thing on my mind was how to put my body to deserving use until the end of time.

He and I met for the first time on a horse-racing track.

This was a dating landscape full of chic and elegant boys and girls, all silently searching for luck in wealth and love. The boys showed off their affluence and the girls advertised their beauty; it was here where a whore was deemed equal to a noble lady, where a virtuous young woman could, in the blink of an eye, develop the desires of a whore, where an entire aristocratic society shamelessly and arrogantly put on display its immoral insanities. Yes, they took the form of authorised casinos, where people left their own human morals up to the God of Fortune to decide. There were hopes of selecting an individual happiness, which would forever revolt against the fundamental morals of the majority; here, humankind revealed its true nature as a bunch of sluts disguising themselves under the pretence of glamour, progress, and civilisation. In this place where upper-class sluts fooled around, who would have the courage to consider the honour of a woman even if I begged for the life of me!

I sat in the opulent grandstand, mixed with men who also put powder and lipstick on their faces like the women, as well as women in bizarre trendy modern outfits that graciously aired out their thighs and chests under thin veils. All the while, my husband fixed his attention on those horse racing betting cards about the Longchamp 2200-metre championship, racking his brain over *Double Évent* and *Triple Évent*, the *Pégasec* and the

Orchidée. Then I noticed a man donning a neat suit—a pair of binoculars hanging on his chest, a Contax camera in hand—his demeanour just like that of a Parisian despite being an Annamite. He had permission to wander on the pebbled yard, with footsteps as measured as those of a veteran in the business of horse racing who no longer had to rack his brain like the rookies already on the edge of their seats even before the race had started. Suddenly, I seemed to recall that when I first stepped foot into the ring, that man took a picture of me. I noticed also that whenever the herd of horses returned, he'd simply lift his camera and quickly press the button, then nod his head as if thoroughly content. He had a special aura to him; throughout the entire race that day, no one felt as classy as him.

As the race came to an end, my husband helped me up, his face as sorrowful as that of a person attending a funeral. He rambled about something I didn't care for. Something about him losing several double championships and some tens of silver, winning only four coins in the *Pari Mutuel*[1]. As we went to the cash desk, he kept scolding himself for being more stupid than a pig. Meanwhile, I paid attention only to that noteworthy man. Seeing that he earned quite a thick pile of banknotes, I felt an

---

[1] Betting between horse race attendees, mediated by the race managers, where a part of the money is used on charity works.

instant respect for him, and found my husband useless and deplorable (even more so when he, my own husband, lost his horse race bets). And so the seed of treason, the idea of deceit, was kindled at that very moment: for I, within only several tens of footsteps, had compared my husband's intelligence to that of a passer-by.

After both of them cashed out, and seeing that all the gamblers had dispersed elsewhere, they suddenly took off their hats and greeted each other, shaking hands. Then my husband introduced us.

'Monsieur Tân, my old classmate... Allow me to present to you my wife.'

I bowed my head to greet him with reverence, and felt a tinge of delight in my heart for some unknown reason—perhaps because 'someone like that' could be my husband's old friend, and that'd reflect highly on me. I let the two of them converse cordially with each other while I silently listened on.

'So what are you doing now?'

That man cackled.

'Why, I've become just another social parasite!'

My husband played along.

'That'd be the best if you could keep it up. I'd love to

live that life, but I can't!'

'Then what did you end up doing?'

'A government official. A national parasite.'

'A national financial parasite[1], I see! That said, time really flies by, doesn't it? It felt like yesterday when we were still in school and bickering with each other like two girls sharing one husband!'

'So how many children have you got?'

'I don't even have a wife, let alone children!'

'Wow, why are you being so picky?'

'Not at all! More like no one wants me!'

Then they started talking about betting on horse races. I had no idea what they were talking about; their conversation was filled with names like Cléopâtre, Orion, Reine Margot, Pacifique, Limier, and so on. I went to the races with my husband to check out what people had been wearing, who was more attractive than me, which ones were the luxuriously dressed, how many took photos of me or seemed to desire me—just general observations like that. I didn't come to gamble, so I tuned out of the conversation. I let them gossip, give each other advice,

---

[1] From the French *budgétivore,* meaning someone who feeds off the national budget.

and make plans. One noteworthy thing, though: the friend was worldly. More cunning and experienced than my husband! By a large margin!

When we made our way to the Parreau causeway[1], there was no car in sight. Just as my husband began to complain, his friend immediately said.

'Alright, I have a car. Allow me to take you two to your front door.'

Then the man walked over to a modern-style sedan, tossed a dime to the kid who watched over the car, opened the door and invited us in like a driver, before getting in the driver's seat himself. I wasn't sure if he went mad because there was a beautiful woman in his car, but he hit 60 even though we were driving in the city, which scared my pants off. When he parked the car in front of our house, I stepped down and said something I thought was very clever.

'I didn't know I was alive in your car this whole time.'

He laughed.

'Dear madame, what's the use of a car if not to go fast? Having said that, I'm always very careful.'

My husband became all fussy.

---

[1] Now Hoàng Hoa Thám street.

'Hey, come in for a sec! Come take a quick look at the house and stuff. We're old friends, right?'

He came in. Elated, I made the tea and grabbed the cigarettes with flustered excitement, for I viewed my husband's old friend as an utterly venerable, esteemed guest. The two of them resumed talking about horse racing for a long while, then decided on joining forces on the next race next Sunday. Upon taking his leave, the friend promised to take his car to pick us up once again.

During dinner later that night, even though my husband was sad for having lost his bet, he was also happy to brag to me about all the good qualities of his old friend with whom he finally reunited after ten years. Thanks to my husband's exaltations, I learned that Tân was the son of an incredibly affluent governor-general, who studied abroad in France, earned a baccalaureate, and never needed a job because his father was renting out up to twenty houses in Hà Nội. Tân married when he was eighteen, divorced her, then went abroad, and hadn't married again after returning from France. Tân kept on living by himself to enjoy every pleasure that life had to offer, my husband concluded.

'The most content man on earth! He has a good reputation, excellent education, great money whilst being free from family life—on top of not having to work for

Westerners! Liberty on all fronts, truly a blessed guy.'

'But he must mess around a lot... Just look at his face.'

'That I'm not certain, since we haven't met in so long... But that must be so. In this day and age, what man doesn't mess around? If a guy in his position doesn't play around, then is he trying to be a God of Preservation?'

That night, as I laid in my husband's embrace, I couldn't ward off the fantasy, the desire, and the vision that I was in Tân's arms. Virginity for my husband? Well, I had already lost it before getting married, didn't I? So, even though no one else knew about it, for me, I must always keep that in mind! Moreover, I had to constantly remind my conscience that my life had already been ruined because of that. To lie to myself that I was pure felt somehow cowardly to me! No, I was no longer pure, and if I tried to deny it to myself, then I'd be damned. As if my pride would allow that! And because I had no longer been a virtuous and noble-minded person for a long time, what should I preserve my morals for? There was no other night like that night, when corruption burgeoned in the mind of a married woman with such justified reasoning.

And such thoughts reminded me of Nguyễn Lưu! Immediately the scene of Lưu's suicide flashed before my eyes, as vividly as if on a screen. His head lolling backward, his mouth smeared with black foam, his eyes slightly open and bloodshot, his entire body strewn on the ground like an ocean wave: the body of a person who loved me, suffered to death for me, he who should've been my husband, taken me in as his lifelong, loyal wife, and granted me the chance to be a pure woman! That man who committed suicide was murdered! And that murderer was none other than the man is now my husband, holding me, an arm sliding under my neck, the other on my chest, one leg solemnly across my stomach! I freed myself from my husband's embrace, pushed that leg off to sit up straight, found my husband despicable and deserving death, and found myself detestable! What a joke! Was I still human or not? How could I live under the same roof with a man like that for so long, and after such awful tragedy? I reached out to turn on the lights, looking over to the space next to me, dazed. Although I had shoved him aside, my husband at that point was still sleeping soundly and was even huddled up, which made him look incredibly sordid. He also snored as loudly as a coolie on rice paddies, with drool streaming from his mouth down onto the mattress. I pouted. I recalled those nights of nasty lovemaking where my husband put even his own tongue to use, how dastardly, how dirtily, how despicably!

Upon hearing the clock beeping twelve dignified notes, I felt chills; the room around me suddenly felt raher too big.

I sat under the blanket next to my husband, yet I found myself lonely, loveless, and yearning for comfort, as if I was the most heartbroken person on earth.

Fatigued, exhausted, and wistful, I let out a long yawn and stretched my shoulders.

Eventually I turned off the lights again, laid down, pulled the blanket over my head, then hugged my husband, who I imagined to be Tân. An affair in thought!

Now the two of you can see how a married woman, a decent and even distinguished woman, in just one night, came to think like a streetwalker and was thus understandably plagued with a troubled mood.

The following Sunday, something urgent came up and my husband had to return to his hometown. Before leaving, my husband reminded me to apologise to Tân, should he come to pick us up in his car as promised. That afternoon, Tân really came over, and fell right into my trap—that is, he stepped into the house just as I was opening my wardrobe to get my áo dài. Just as my lily-white skin flickered underneath the thin veil of my blouse still creased with corset lines, so did my underwear... Tân was startled and dumbfounded like any other man would've found himself. I set this up because my mind was influenced by those newspapers: every day they'd discuss heatedly about movie stars, European and American makeup looks, how Marlène Dietrich drew her eyebrows, how Crawford exuded sexual allure, which people innocently and unabashedly defined as 'sex appeal'. So what I did was simply show off my sex appeal like a star—no big deal!

I lowered my head in response to Tân's greetings, then turned back to the wardrobe to find my clothes, taking my sweet time so that Tân could freely observe my... 'sex appeal' behind my back. After a long while, I eventually put my áo dài on and turned around.

'Dear sir, please take a seat.'

Tân stammered,

'Madame, is your husband not in?'

'No, my husband has urgent business to take care of back home, so he told me to send you his apologies.'

Tân stood there for some time, hesitant, then said.

'I guess I'll have to go by myself then.'

'Yes, but please take a seat and have a drink, sir.'

'Oh no, please allow me to take my leave...'

Tân still stood there despite having said that. I didn't

move either as I stared at him, unsure whether I should receive my husband's friend when he was absent! Finally, Tân walked straight out of the house as I didn't invite him to stay again.

As I sat by myself, I felt a surge of joy. I'd made a person want me; I'd captivated him for three minutes, by sexual provocation... No, my '*sex appeal*' would be better, for if I were to say it in our mother tongue, it'd lose all of its poetic appeal and artistic value. It would instead become promiscuous by local standards, even though it meant the same thing in both languages. The mystery of languages, of nouns! All hail those 'writers' of cinema!

During dinner later that day, my husband and I were at each other's throats due to my 'negligence' while receiving Tân. He mumbled with a mouthful of food.

'How embarrassing of you to have done that! I can't believe it!'

'What? That was as far as any reception would go, wasn't it? Be reasonable, will you?'

'Oh, you shut your trap—stop talking back to me! He was so polite, he even drove his car to pick me up. I'd already agreed to meet him, yet you keep talking back to me like that, so much so that even a dog wouldn't hold back from barking at you!'

'But what do you expect me to do since you weren't home?'

'Then just humour him with some more hospitality—what's the big deal? Are you a country bumpkin? Have you always been this dumb? Have you never been with a guest by yourself before?'

'But we aren't close yet.'

'He's an old friend, don't you get it?'

'But he's rich! I don't want to look like I'm licking his boots!'

'Shut up, you nitwit! Are we asking for favours just because he's rich? If you keep talking like that I'd rather talk to a rock!'

'Get a grip, you! Stop imposing your views on me!'

'You get a grip—stop pulling that equality talk! If that's what modernity looks like, then what a shame—what a waste of this so-called modernity! A modern woman who can't politely receive her husband's friend, so ignorant that she doesn't take the blame for her husband when he makes a mistake... And she can't even invite him to have a drink or a cigarette!'

'That's what you get for a bumpkin like me!'

'That's why you need to shut up, you nitwit!'

From that time until the next day, my husband and I were in a silent war, not breathing a word in each other's direction. Silently I was euphoric, because if Tân came by in the future, I would've had absolute freedom to act without any worries about raising my husband's suspicions. It turned out that with just a little strategic obedience, you could get anything you want in life. Without admitting to my old mistake, I quietly fixed my behaviour. One month later, after interacting with Tân a few more times, when our social interactions sufficed to coat us in an air of intimacy, my husband happened to be absent one Sunday morning. Tân dropped by anyway. I was naturally and familiarly conversing with my husband's precious friend just like he wanted. In two hours, we had talked about everything there was to talk about, and if Administrateur Kim could've eavesdropped on how freely this speech had flowed, he'd surely wish for his wife to remain an old-fashioned woman for the rest of her life!

In between some mundane topics, Tân chanced upon an opportunity to confide in me his thoughts and feelings... Ah, I now saw that this was the beginning of every end where a man and a woman would finally get caught in the trap of love. When I implied that I found Tân too nitpicky, he said sullenly,

'You're misunderstanding me. I've never nitpicked without a good reason. The fact that I'm not married even now is because my perspective on love is drastically different from the majority.'

I laughed heartily, half-joking, half-serious.

'Ah, so brother Tân is getting philosophical! Terrific. I'd love to hear what you have to say.'

'Yes, you're correct. I don't consider marriage the end goal of love. Don't you see how many people obsess over each other, but the moment they get married, they grow bored of each other and fall out of love? Being together for life is only a formality, whilst love is the real ideal. And you can't confine an ideal into rules and boundaries. What's more, if you get married only to fall out of love, then it'd be better not to get married. You'll perpetually suffer in your longing for each other, which means you'll only love each other all the more so!'

'If that's how you think, how could any woman dare to love you?'

Then, Tân stood up, dropped his arms, and sighed.

'And so that's my agony. Dignified women aside, even those streetwalkers can't evoke a feeling of love in me any more.'

'Why is that?'

'Because they keep wanting me to marry them. They don't understand that I'm terrified of marriage. Once you become husband and wife, you'll definitely end up treating each other like crap. Mrs. Kim, my belief that marriage damages love parallels a religious devotee's belief in God.'

'But why would someone like you want to love streetwalkers?'

Tân sat down, his face stern, and returned with a question.

'Why not? When you love someone, you have to leave the past behind. I can love streetwalkers because I believe that there's no virginity in this world—spiritually speaking. Never, ever, would a man get to love a girl who never had a secret crush on anyone before him, even just for an hour, or even a minute. In fact, if we were to consider the virginity of the mind as worthy—as opposed to the body—what wrong have streetwalkers ever done? Being loved by a streetwalker brings me more love than an aristocrat. That's why I love them. Only streetwalkers know how to compare and contrast because they're veterans in the business of men's opinions. This makes their love even more valuable and undisputed. I believe I've made my case clear to you.'

I pondered, then answered,

'You have really strange ideas.'

Weary, Tân stood up.

'Perhaps I'm crazy. Just look at me: ever since I became an adult, I have been tormented by love. I loved that woman and married her, but then marriage wrecked our love to the point that she became insolent towards me, so much so that we parted ways! And it wasn't because she cheated on me. You must understand that to see through the dangers of marriage. Since then, life has been so boring to me...'

I cackled, finding words to console him.

'And yet my husband always praises you for being the happiest man on earth.'

'He's mistaken, too!'

He grabbed his hat to signal his departure, then continued,

'Me, the happiest man on earth? I was ruined by love the moment I became an adult. I got tangled up in the marriage business and never had the chance to live a mundane life like everyone else! For these past ten years, that wound has not once closed up. I was under so many influences that I had no desire to continue my studies; I did nothing of note and only mindlessly messed around. Just look at me: I have money, health, status, even a bit of education, yet I'm never happy. I have everything, but not even a single speck of love! I even went all the way to the West, only to find no woman at all! Besides, how could I have? It seems like everyone already has their own destined path. Well! The person I wanted to love didn't get to love me, and only people I don't love desperately want to be in a relationship! Love must come with mutual understanding... And mutual understanding isn't as easy as people think, because the concept of 'understanding' differs greatly for me in comparison to others. Anyway, since your husband has been taking a while, I'd like to take my leave here.'

Then, Tân shook my hand and left. Every time he stopped by or left the residence, his car engine revved just like my anticipating heart.

From then on, sometimes I took advantage of my husband's injections at my uncle's house to ask Tân to come visit. After seeing his wife behaving as cool, calm, and collected like a true modern girl, which meant boldly humouring Tân with great intimacy, my husband appeared delighted, and even complimented me.

'Good job, that's more like it! Tu es devenue très femme du monde!'

Then he awarded me with a smacking kiss.

Indeed, he had no suspicion whatsoever! He had no idea that what was in disguise was already as clear as day: for Tân kept coming over for meals and inviting me to parties; for Tân and I would miss each other when we were out of sight, even though neither spoke a word about our feelings. As for my husband, he could never in his wildest dreams entertain the tragedy of his friend and his wife, and simply saw it as an opportunity to brag to the world that he had a friend with a car who frequently picked him up. Besides, if I kept up my cunning front, there was no room for jealousy for any husband!

After our mingling carried on for a month, Tân asked my husband one day to give me permission to visit Tam Thanh with one of his lady friends.

'Brother Kim, she's the wife of a friend of mine who passed away. She's been a widow for these past six years yet she lives on just like that, revering her husband and raising her children without fail. She wanted me to take her on a forest sightseeing trip with my car, which I promised but never had the chance. So please allow your wife to come with us, so that two women can keep the other's company on the road, and that people won't gossip about our friendship...'

Without giving it any second thought, my husband

cheerfully said,

'Mais avec grand plaisir.'

Tân spoke firmly once more.

'If you don't have to go to work, I'd love to invite both of you. But my lady friend can't wait until the weekend, for the trip from Ninh Bình to Hà Nội would take only a few days.'

My husband nodded fervently again.

'Sure! Sure thing!'

'So, Madame Administrateur, please get ready at seven tomorrow morning. I'll drive to your place, you'll get acquainted with Mrs. Hội over a cup of warm water, then we'll head off right away, alright? It'll take about three hours one way and four hours to visit the cave, so we'll get back to Hà Nội by around late afternoon tomorrow.'

'Sounds good! And since I'm entrusting my wife to you, you've got to be careful while driving, okay? Lạng Sơn road is full of jungles and mountains, so you shouldn't be speeding too recklessly...'

'Have no fear, my friend! If you have an excellent car, there's nothing to worry about. Dear madame, would you kindly agree to this arrangement?'

Nonchalantly, I replied,

'Yes.'

Tân took his leave, then, when we entreated him to stay, said,

'No can do; you must let me go right now, for I have much to prepare. I have to buy some canned food, then set up my film roll to take commemorative photos! So, goodbye to you both, and see you tomorrow morning.'

And thus my husband and I got into an argument again. I was the one initiating it, for reasons that I need not elaborate. Even though I was elated on the inside, toward my husband, I still objected.

'What's with you? How can you be so easy?'

My husband stood dumbfounded for a while, then asked,

'What? You don't want to go? I thought you weren't busy tomorrow?'

'It's not about being busy. It's that the trip is so long and you aren't coming, which makes things very inconvenient!'

'What's inconvenient about it when there are three of you?'

'But it feels weird to me!'

'Because you're old-fashioned, that's why!'

'You should've at least asked me first whether I wanted to go. Why did you agree so easily and readily?'

'If I didn't agree right away, then wouldn't that mean I'm suspicious of my friend? That I think you're indecent? A sceptic man is a jealous man. That's a shameful way to live! Now that we're living a new life like the West, we mustn't suspect each other in the old-fashioned way. I thought it'd be fine even if I let you go by yourself with Tân. It wouldn't be polite to let you have a say in it, because you'd immediately reject him!'

'Stop it. There's a limit to how civilised you should be.'

My husband slammed his hand on the table and shouted,

'You stop it. There's a limit to how old-fashioned you should be, too! Stop talking, you nitwit! The more your husband trusts and cherishes you, the more you berate him?'

I quickly apologised. Then, ten minutes later, the two of us were giddy again, kissing and smooching like kids. Every so often, a wife who was about to cheat or had already cheated would suddenly be struck with unexpected moments of inspiration. They would compel her to love her husband with even more passion when the seeds of betrayal budded within her, and so after he got to scold me for being a nitwit—which happened very rarely—he had me hug and kiss him dearly. He was on cloud nine, vigorously reciprocating my words of love just like on our consummation night. Embracing that head slick and shiny with scented wax, I found my husband truly flawless; in my personal opinion, a flawless husband must be a carefree husband with absolute faith in his wife, blind in both eyes as well as deaf in both ears. Or, if not blind and deaf, then he at least must allow opportunities for his wife to cheat! It turned out that my husband met all of these conditions, and even had said qualities in an extremely subtle and sophisticated manner.

The next morning, I woke up early. My body was well rested, my spirit beaming with a love for life, and my face was fresh like a flower lightly watered with spring rain. I'd spent the entire night before mulling over which makeup this trip deserved, so it took me only about half an hour in front of the mirror to transform into an especially fashionable fairy. Dear me! Surely Tân must be astounded to see how much more beautiful I was today compared to other days! Now, let's see if that Mrs. Hội something was still a young woman, if she was prettier than me. And whether she was Tân's secret lover or a genuine lady friend of his! I was getting jealous for no reason—already I was inflicted with this. Coupled with novel-like fantasies about the promise of poetically delightful natural landscapes, of jungles and mountains, of wind and clouds, of caves and passes, of streams and rivers, this man, with his car, his camera—who respected me deeply—would surely love me once we reached Tam Thanh, even if he had not fallen for me just yet. This abundance of fantasies about our clandestine affair seemed to have manifested on my face, coating me with a particularly invigorated aura of a woman waited on by love. And if my husband were to catch on to me then, he would've been shocked by my enthusiasm for going out, even though I had just caused a ruckus with him the night before.

Ah! The buzzing of a car. Tân was here! Ah, Mrs. Hội! Damn, that velvet shirt looked really nice! She seemed young too—not shabby at all! They entered... Oh! Administrateur Kim still hadn't finished tying his shoelaces! They came in...

'My greetings to you both.'

'My pleasure! Please come in, madame.'

'Great, the lady has finished getting ready! I would've been worried out of my mind if she had still been doing her face!'

After saying that, Tân pointed to a chair for Hội to sit down. I poured out a few cups of lotus tea, and slid a box of matches and a packet of Camel cigarettes toward Tân. Mrs. Hội craned her neck forward and said,

'What a shame. I wish it were your day off, because it'd be great fun to have you with us.'

My husband, having finished tying his shoelaces, stood up and replied.

'It's truly a great pity.'

At that moment, the private driver was already walking out in measured steps, his hat held tightly in front of his chest. My husband looked up at the clock, then hurriedly said,

'Oh, crap! It's almost noon. My apologies to you both, my boss told me to come in early today—how very unfortunate!'

And then my flawless husband happily left.

After three hours, the car had manoeuvred around the coasts in the Lạng province. I witnessed what a jungle road looked like! The twists and turns that seemed to run backward to us, the circular and triangle warning signs for dangerous turns, the herds of ginormous white buffaloes squished against each other and against the slope of the mountain upon hearing the car honk. There were Hmong men who avoided the car with much more fear and care than Kinh people, ancient trees on the side of the road, rock cliffs protruding from the mountains above the car as if threatening to collapse, streams down under abyssal chasms where water of different colours wouldn't mix. There were also huge and peculiar water wheels, delectable stilt houses flickering in between reed bushes, vines clinging onto sky-high precipices all the way on the top of the mountain, and muddy black clouds plagued with death stuck on the incline. Genuinely speaking, even though these images flashed by the windows on both sides of the car like brief documentary clips on a screen, they always remained vivid in my mind. Why so? Because my 'driver' had on a sky-blue Mossant hat, with a mountaineering-style outfit, a white pair of gloves made from deer skin; and he was an excellent driver. Despite accelerating the car near deadly speeds, we came out unscathed, which made me want to stand up, put my arms around his neck, and award him with a few pecks, if Mrs. Hội hadn't been dozing off next to me. That day, Tân appeared in my eyes not only as a talented and intelligent individual worthy of being called a proper man, but also something akin to a hero. As I thought that, I remembered Nguyễn Lưu, a poor student, so young yet so old-fashioned like a geezer—not to mention his inability to enjoy all the pleasures in life.

These men were as different from each other as chalk and cheese, and yet I was in love once again! To think that I hadn't known a single thing back then, still so wet behind the ears and reckless with my first love. That trip to the Lạng province by car and the visit to the caves on foot were nothing to write home about. Stories explaining the history, tradition, and words of praise and criticism for the Creator made up the majority of the trip. As I tested the waters, it seemed that Tân and Hội were likely just friends. I began harbouring feelings of love for Tân. But I had to remain subtle enough so that Hội wouldn't raise any questions.

I regretted not being able to brush aside my thirst for love, which made me blurt out things I didn't mean to say. I would sometimes even slip up around Hội, and because of this worry, my spirit wasn't fully present to enjoy the natural landscape. They took photos, picked up colourful pebbles and exotic fruits, filling up their overcoat pockets. Then they plunged their hands in the river and played around like children; they led each other around, stepped around on the rocks, then cackled as they nearly slipped and fell. And then when we came back to Lạng province, we dropped by to visit Hội's uncle. I sat yawning in the living room so Hội could have a private conversation with her family members while Tân went out to refill the car with petrol. Then there were gifts sent out from the mountains, conversations about antlers, tiger bone glue, snakes, bear bile, then a series of invitations and rejections, loads and loads of complicated formalities, which wasted infinitely more time... I found myself oddly bored, for the car had turned southward once more. I almost concluded that the trip was bland, if Tân hadn't parked the car to have dinner before arriving at Phủ Lạng Thương[1].

We found a grassy hill surrounded by a rather fine view, which was also near the main road so that we could watch over the car. Tân opened the trunk on the back of the car and pulled out a gargantuan package. He laid a big cloth on top of the grass, then put out a full course: a luxurious feast! Pig thigh, pig tongue, fried fish in tomato sauce, goose liver, bread... even a kilogram of ripe grapes and a bottle of red wine. Before we dined, Tân told Hội and me to lie on my side on the grass and raise our glasses so that he could take a few more film photos, to remember this unforgettable meal.

Hội asked,

'This is what they call... a picnic, right, Tân?'

'Dear sister, that is correct. While our meal is lacking many dishes, the taste would surely be better than to dine

---

[1] Now known as Bắc Giang province.

at home!'

'Oh, definitely so... Now we know: what is hard to gain and difficult to find is truly precious.'

The ways in which Tân catered to and cared for the two of us were extraordinarily commendable. Even as a waiter or a driver, Tân always carried himself with poetic passion. I then grew sceptical of Hội, thinking that if she had a friend like Tân, she'd be dumb not to fall for him. There must've been some secrets behind their relationship.

As the feast came to an end and the afternoon grew darker, Tân told us two women to go take some photos so that he could use up his entire roll of thirty-two shots. But Hội asked if she could have a nap, for she was unbearably tired. She then lay on the grass and actually fell asleep, leaving me by myself with Tân, strolling around to find a cluster of flowers, a tree trunk...

As we had each other to ourselves, we found a piece of rock suitable for a couple to sit side by side. The landscape felt like a partner in crime. After some aimless rambling, Tân casually struck up a conversation.

'So, you see, my life always seems to be lacking something. Watching this scenery and getting to dine with my friends like this, I should be content, yet I suddenly feel even more melancholic and miserable.'

I gazed into the distance, as if speaking to no one.

'Life without love really is depressing, huh?'

Tân's face became stern.

'Especially when the person you love has no idea how much you're suffering.'

Before I could answer, Tân took hold of my hands. His voice was strangely sincere, oddly pitiful...

'Please allow me to say this! Whatever it is, please let me finish my thoughts... There's nothing more miserable than having to hide your deepest thoughts from everyone.'

'...'

'I'm telling the truth. I've fallen in love with you, Huyền. Now that I've gathered the courage to say this, that means I've pondered over it plenty. To love your friend's wife, or to have a lover when you already have a husband—what a blasphemous thing to do. Yet in this world, the number of those who have no other choice but to cheat is in the hundreds of millions! We can't help it, for when the heart wavers, the mind must concede.'

'...'

'If you cannot love me, then that means you cannot

love your own husband, and that Huyền's happiness no longer lies within loyalty...'

As I kept staring at the tips of my shoes, Tân lifted my hand toward his lips for a kiss. Seeing my lack of resistance, Tân slowly pulled me into a tight embrace and kissed me on the lips: a kiss that was in no way ordinary, but rather a special kiss through which we found a happiness akin to being able to drink in each other's souls. It was a victorious kiss of love against duty, our heartbeats thumping to this ode to joy—a kiss like those in the movies, where I felt as if I'd entrusted my entire body to that person! The contract had thus been signed by both parties. Such a kiss had brought on the final assault on the life of a woman who had only a few rookie morality soldiers in her fortress of conscience.

Out of fear of raising suspicion, we rushed to wake up Hội and implored her to get in the car, despite knowing how rude it was for us to do so. We were home that very afternoon. My husband was elated, because the trip itself posed many threats and yet I returned safe and sound and 'completely unscathed'. Hội was happy, too: she went to Lang basically to seek financial assistance from her uncle and received positive responses. Doling out touching words of gratitude, my husband saw Tân off.

Just like that, I got to enjoy the pleasures that my

husband only kindled in me but never bothered to satisfy. After my instances of infidelity, I pampered my husband even more, so the more the husband was deceived by his wife, the more he came to trust her.

The affair dragged on for months on end while we never feared causing a ruckus, to the point that I personally thought it'd last for a lifetime. The car was truly a magical object. It saved time. It was also a wonderfully private chamber.

Indeed, there were many times when we enjoyed the tantalising pleasure of sex in its most complete and comprehensive form in that sedan, on main roads five kilometres away from the city on moonlit nights—or on starless nights at empty junctures by a cotton tree or a chinaberry tree surrounded by a vast and endless field... who could tell? Tân parked the car on the sideway, turned on a small light on the back, then a blue headlight, and then what came after was... from 'do you love me' to 'my dear, kiss me!' Oftentimes we finished our lovemaking before the car even had the chance to cool down completely after parking. And then—brr brr brr—Tân turned the car around again, accelerated to 100 to return to Hà Nội, and told Kim that the two of us were out buying some stuff in town. The husband checked the clock and, seeing that the wife didn't take even more than half an hour, even gave them compliments!

'You didn't take any time at all, even with all that business to take care of. What a convenience a car is!'

Tân and I snuck a glance at each other and smiled.

I lived happy days that I could never forget. I viewed my deception of my husband as nothing sinful, only romantic and novel-like, with a little bit of a cinematic flair to it. And the more he betrayed his friend, the more Tân acted amiably through expensive methods, suddenly rendering Kim as someone who unknowingly procured his own wife for his personal benefits.

But one day...

That secret affair had run its course. Public opinion had worn off its benevolence. Out of the blue, intuition guided a slim ray of light into the cuckold's foolish mind. The cheaters had reached the point of reckless complacency, as they slipped out of the frying pan and into the fire, after having thought that society consisted of only the deaf or the blind...

And thus Huyền began approaching the most abject period of her life.

IV - Debauchery

That afternoon, for no reason whatsoever, my husband crossed his arms and asked me solemnly,

'Do you know what a woman's happiness is in this civilised day and age, Huyền?'

Startled, I did not understand why my husband suddenly asked me that question. Then I got flustered, desperate to answer right away though I was unable to; fear was written all over my face. Catching my suspicious expression red-handed, my husband laughed bitterly.

'Huyền can't answer me? I thought that question wasn't difficult in the slightest. Oh, my dearest Huyền whom I love most in this world, if you can't answer me, then let me do it for you, okay? It's very simple! Here: a woman's happiness in this civilised day and age is to have a husband who possesses wealth and prestige, who loves and pampers her with absolution, only for her to cuckold him!'

With that, I was done for! My body went cold as if it had fallen into a river in the middle of winter. Those words, uttered with tenderness and measuredness, unexpectedly exerted a power so formidable that I had no wits left to open my mouth and utter a single word. I lowered my head instead, exactly as if I was confessing to my sins. I never imagined my husband would abruptly and swiftly catch me off guard like that, and so I didn't have time to prepare... I couldn't do anything to prevent my face from turning pale, my heart from pounding, my limbs from trembling... Truly, I was done for! From that moment on, he had the upper hand to condemn me to his heart's content. That day, the house was empty as the nanny and the private driver were ordered elsewhere by my husband. He didn't have to watch his words for any fly on the wall.

'You bastard! Confess! How many times have you slept with Tân? Huyền! I have been treating you so well—have I ever done anything wrong for you to deceive me like this?'

I lowered my head and kept my silence for three minutes straight before coming up with only one question.

'Who told you that?'

'You don't need to know! What you should know is whether you should feel ashamed of your conscience! What do you have to say about that, you bastard! You two-timer! Speak up!'

'Stop being jealous for no reason... I hung out with Tân because you forced me to! It was against my will! Even if I did cheat, it's all your fault!'

Before I could finish, a spiteful punch struck my face, sending me flying onto the floor... I blacked out. When I woke up again, I was properly laid on a bed. My husband sat next to me, scribbling away with a pencil on a white sheet of paper clipped to the cover of a big book on a pillow. Noticing my eyes opening, he stopped and asked,

'You had the gall to say "even if"? You want me to spell out the evidence that's already as clear as day, don't you? You want to look bad, I'll give it to you. Do you want me to spell it out to you? Huyền!'

He paused for some time, then went on wailing again.

'What a devastating lesson for the foolish, over trusting husbands, including me! I'm also a good-for-nothing, but for me to be called a good-for-nothing when I love you is no reason for you to deceive me and sleep around with another good-for-nothing man!'

Up to this point I had still been in shock... one side

of my face was aching with pain. My jaw felt as if it had dislocated, and my teeth felt like they would fall out. Then I was paralysed with utter terror! How... how could my husband suddenly act so curtly and crudely? If I were to talk back with a few more stubborn words, how far would his cruelty go? And then I realised right away: the benevolent ones were always the curt ones! If that was the case, then I should employ the silent treatment—so silent that it could grow to be a resentment so great where I wouldn't even bother responding, rather than having the urge to reply without knowing how. Women's best course of action toward men, in cases such as mine, had always been silence, if not resorting to tears. Once the accusation was correct, then the objection must be skilfully handled if we wish to delude the judge into believing that we were framed. Though I had unintentionally kept silent before, I could plant in his mind a seed of scepticism if I approached this more strategically—if luck were on my side. As I thought of that, I buried my face in my cotton pillow.

But, alas! My husband had all the damning evidence!

'Last Saturday, at seven thirty, you told me you were going out to buy some shirt buttons. Then you called a cab to Paul Bert flower garden[1]. There, Tân's car was

---

[1] Now Indira Gandhi flower garden.

already waiting for you! The two of you sped through Sông Cái bridge, then took an unknown turn. At nine, that car dropped you off at Hàng Đậu flower garden, let you call a cab back home first, and then only half an hour later did Tân come invite me to mahjong, is that right? What do you have to say to that?'

My soul was completely knocked out of my body! Those accusations were absolutely spot on. Unable to work out an objection, I had no other choice but to keep my face planted to my pillow. Feeling no need for a useless objection, in that dire moment, I could only wonder who had busted my affair into oblivion despite its extreme secrecy!

My husband continued.

'This Thursday, he picked you up at the "Memorial Monument"[1] and dropped you off at the Grand Palais Maurice Long after you two screwed on a road near Kim Liên. His car is nothing but a brothel! Your steamy sessions had been protected by that secretive brothel up until now! All this time, you've slept around with him at least a few dozens of times! And each time took just one or two hours! How modern of you! How upper class of you! Is that right? Answer me! I'm speaking to you!'

---

[1] A location in front of Hà Nội Flagtower.

I wanted to hold it in but couldn't anymore. My husband brutally gripped my hair and jerked me up. Words of reproach, interrogation, and resentment incessantly slapped me in the face like a downpour. When I had to sit up, I was still wobbling on my feet—my husband pushed me off the bed and shoved me down the stairs! At this point, I came to understand that there was no use in talking back, yet silence wouldn't solve anything, either! Really, it was over! It was time for my fate to rebel against me! After indecent sessions of pleasure that showed us maddening ecstasy, it was now time for my punishment.

'I'm begging you, I beg you a thousand times over! I'm really a worthless woman—please forgive me!'

Strangely, my husband acted nonchalantly and threw no more angry fits, he only nodded and spoke gleefully.

'That's more like it! You're being very reasonable now. If you had continued to talk back, we'd have problems! Just keep kneeling like that and listen up!'

I was too terrified to glance up to see what my husband was up to. Amidst my mental turmoil, tears flooded down my cheeks. After some time, my husband said.

'Do you know what your life will be like from now on? Huyền!'

'I can only beg to rely on your chivalrous heart, your

forgiveness for a worthless woman like me, that is all...'

I broke down in tears again. Devastated, I regretted not having thought far enough—if I kept on lying to my husband, then even the most benign and foolish husband would have every right to berate, torment, and tarnish me. Before, I had thought that losing my virginity wasn't that big of a deal and my husband wouldn't have made such a big fuss about it. In this world, how often would you come across a cuckolded husband who carried on and loved his wife just as before, one who lacks the courage to torture her despite his own wrath? The miserable thing was that this husband was neither benign nor loving toward his wife like those other husbands!

He said,

'So? Let's get a divorce, shall we? Would you like that? How about I take you back to your house and tell your parents all about your shameful deeds? Then I'll take you to court and make you admit to your crimes to the judges! Then you can go marry whoever you want and go fuck whoever you wish!'

That'd be a death sentence! That'd be committing suicide! If my parents were to find out about me like this, then I couldn't keep on living! Dear Heavens! I actually had a father and a mother! I hadn't done anything to repay them, so how could I be living so dishonourably to humiliate them like this? Why did I only remember my parents now? What would become of my father? Would my mother be able to live on? Oh, dear Heavens... I clasped my hands together like I was in front of a Buddha statue, pleading and yelping with utmost devastation.

'No, don't divorce me!'

My husband shrugged his shoulders.

'Then what would you like, dear madame? Do you want to keep reigning over this house like a domestic general and be this fool's "most precious wife on earth" forever, or what? After all those filthy betrayals, you still think you haven't done enough damage to my reputation that you still want to "mother" me some more, dear madame?'

Taking a long time to consider, I finally collapsed to my husband's feet, rambling.

'Dear husband, I know I've done something stupid. I've turned out this way because I've misunderstood those two words: civilisation and socialisation... If you can look at it from that perspective, if you can still show generosity to a gullible and repentant girl, then please spare me your pity...'

'Right! I can do that. I'd like you to keep your lips sealed about this shame on my name, and for your sake, too, especially yours! And then what? Do you know what punishment is most deserving for monstrous women like you—do you know? You thought that civilisation and socialisation meant lying to your husband and sleeping around with men? Listen up: from now on, you'll live a life of misery and shame if you don't want me to wrap you up in banana leaves and walk you out the door... Yes, you'll be considered a housemaid, a servant... You'll no longer have any authority of a wife! I can respect a girl at that brothel in Yên Thái alley but not you, for the truth is that what you've done is ten times more disgusting than prostitution... That means you're lucky if I can spare any pity for you, so don't whine or don't complain about it no matter how vicious my treatment. You must keep at it forever and ever, until my anger subsides, until I can forget—then you can stop. So, you must promise me that much if you don't want a divorce. How does that sound?'

Without giving it a second thought, I placed my bet.

'Yes—gladly so! With a sin like mine, no matter what punishment and admonition come my way, I have to grit my teeth through it. So that you can witness a woman's regret and repentance.'

'Good! That's enough, stand up!'

Meekly, I stood up, having no breathing room to consider that submission was even more humiliating than my affair. My husband took a seat at the table, pointed to the opposite chair for me to sit down, pushed toward me the sheet of paper with chicken scratch in pencil, then continued,

'Once you're done reading, copy this word by word onto another piece of paper, then sign your name at the end. We must at least have written evidence. I'm no fan of empty words! Now, read this!'

> '*A few words of confession.*
>
> *By writing these lines and signing my name underneath, as the first wife and official wife of Mr..., I hereby confess to the crime of deceiving my husband and cheating multiple times with my husband's friend, Tân. I have wasted a great fortune of my husband's money with my lover on lavish indulgences. As my schemes were brought to light, my husband wanted a divorce, yet I wished not to. Therefore, I must repent for my sins and gladly write these words pleading my husband not to be so cruel as to divorce me, and rather to try to spare me his pity so that my life would not later end up in the slums. I guarantee that I will not strive to gain the rights of a first wife, unless my husband reconsiders and allows me to have them. This paper shall serve as proof of that. I am writing this out of my own volition and not due to my husband's imposition. It is only with*

this testimonial will I escape divorce; I will escape revealing a shameful thing to the world, and avoid insulting my own parents.

Hà Nội, date ... month ... year ...

Signature and fingerprint

...'

Having finished reading the letter, I feared I might get trapped in some scheme my conniving husband cooked up. What if I was still forced to get divorced even after signing this humiliating confession? But I dared not hesitate, because I'd reached a dead end already, and beggars couldn't be choosers now. I just pleaded to him to leave out the part about me and my lover wasting a great fortune of my husband's money, for it was a false accusation. Yet my husband frowned.

'Never! You must copy it verbatim; no word out of line. I should at least have some sort of weapon to deal with the man who seduced my wife, don't I? How about that? If you don't want to write that in, fine! We're done!'

Then he grabbed the piece of paper and sprung up. Horrified, I quickly pulled him back.

'Yes, I will write everything in its entirety.'

'Hurry up!'

And so I sat, copying those scathing accusations like a machine, like a person who had nothing to lose. After I was done, my husband tucked the paper in his coat pocket, grabbed a hat, and left. Before going out, he said again,

'Alright! Done! Thank you! From now on, you'll live a different life... I'll let you get onto that bed and under the covers to give it some thought, if you have to.'

Then, the private driver returned. He called him upstairs into the room and ordered,

'The madame is tired! You watch over the house and tell the nanny to prepare dinner!'

And my husband left for good. To where? I had no idea! What would he use that confession for? I had no idea. Did he go look for his rival? Did he go to court? Or to his wife's parents? I had no clue at all! I wanted to find out, but still I had to keep burying myself under the covers. I would be too embarrassed to feel the air entering my lungs, the sunlight shining my way, to look at my face as it was reflected in the mirror, or the driver, the nanny— or even the first pedestrian I'd encounter outside. I'd even be ashamed to look at the greenery around me!

It seemed like everyone had the right to scorn me. It

was only a matter of time before the matter leaked out.

For ten days, I was bedridden, not due to sickness, but something akin to a terminal illness. I was terrified of the humiliation and self-loathing regret that my conscience suffered, to the point that pangs of pain throbbed in my soul. I was more exhausted and restless than a physical wound could ever make me feel. Every day, my husband would come home four times, dish out some niceties toward his wife in front of the servants, but he would never bother to breathe my way when no one was watching. As for me, I was sobbing with my cotton blanket for ten whole days... Oh dear, how could the price to pay for an affair be so costly! After I had my fill of carnal pleasure, now I ached in spirit. Who pushed me to this point? Who put me and Tân under the spell of love?

Was it not my husband? Yes, my husband, with his civilised ideas of coddling his wife like Westerners and provoking her like a lustful demon?

In the downfall of a wife, the husband had at least some responsibility, if not all. And, if so, why was I the only one who had to suffer punishment? At this thought, I resented life, convinced that I did nothing wrong. But fortunately, I cooled down instantly... Why did I say my husband wasn't suffering as well? A cuckold deceived by his wife—surely that was very painful! And so for a period that felt as long as centuries, I went from blaming myself to blaming my husband, pitying myself then pitying my husband, only to end up deeply regretful. Then I knew I had no feelings for Tân. It was a strictly physical relationship. Indeed, in those moments of utter torture, not one resentful and bitter thought against my lover crossed my mind.

On the eleventh day, as I sat to look at myself in the mirror, I was horrified to see an entirely different person. My eyes were sunken, my cheeks hollow, while my skin, once even more pristine than snow, was now pale like a drowned woman. My past beauty, the allure that harmed people and harmed even myself had now vanished into thin air, leaving only the repulsive marks of a filthy, stinky two-timer. Delirious, I forced a smile. The mirror revealed a bizarrely vacant and disagreeable smile. Genuinely speaking, if I'd come to this, to the point where even I felt disgusted by myself, then what husband could spare any love for me? If my husband somehow fell in love with me again, then he'd only be a deplorable fool! What could I hope for in this case?

While I was concerning myself with the future, in deep despair because of this miserable life caged in a mental prison, the old nanny brought a bucket of water in for me.

'How's it going, nanny? How has my husband been these few days?'

Without any knowledge that the male head's wife had just experienced a most cruel tempest, that bumpkin nanny replied without batting an eye.

'What did you say? Nothing's been going on with my master!'

'Those few days when I was sick, did he go out a lot?'

'He went out every night.'

'Have there been visitors to the house recently?'

'Only monsieur Tân, who dropped by a few times.'

'How many times?'

'A couple of times or three, I'm not sure. Dear madame, are you well now? Can you go downstairs now? And why haven't I seen you take any medicine?'

'I've been taking Western medicine, so how could you have known! Anyway, take your leave now.'

What did this mean? Tân must've had no clue that we had been exposed, so that's why he brazenly kept showing up to this house. But why did my husband continue to receive him? What did he want, that seemingly benign but actually incredibly devious man? What was his true goal, when he hadn't left his cheating wife or cut ties with his lying friend? What horrors was my husband scheming? I found no plausible answers to these questions. Suddenly these thoughts sent shivers down my spine. Especially when he'd discovered that secretive affair with such clear evidence. Who had reported us? Where did my husband go to uncover the truth? How does he know it like the back of his hand? Oh, secrets!

Then I must meet Tân for a final time, no matter what! Yes, I must meet my lover to let him know that from now on, we must cut ties—even detest each other for the rest of our lives. The situation had escalated to such a degree. If he'd learned to fear my husband's blistering revenge, Tân wouldn't dare show his face at my house anymore, not when my husband was so incomprehensible. I'd tell Tân: beware! Look out! Your car's about to head to a dangerous turn!

After putting on my makeup, quite half-heartedly, I suddenly found myself wondering: did I need my husband's permission? Right—if I left in silence, I'd be an unrepentant, irredeemable woman. If I asked for my husband's permission, I'd carry out a noble and justified act: to meet Tân and put an end to that indecent love. But would my husband understand it as such? Or would he forbid me on all fronts?

Eventually, I left in silence. If I truly felt regret without any lingering feelings, I surely wouldn't need to meet Tân again. Yet that plan to cut ties was itself yet another piece of evidence of our love affair! And so, to ask for my husband's permission wasn't a recommended course of action. Even if I continued this with Tân or not, I'd keep on living a life under my husband's chiding without change.

That day, I only left when the day began to darken. Approaching Tân's manor-like house, I saw his car in the garage. The roses on the fence did not greet me with their usual bright colours. From upstairs, a ray of light shone through the crack of a door, a wave of sentimental and saccharine music blasting into the air. Gently I pushed the iron gate and quietly walked across the pebbled courtyard, tiptoed on the wooden spiral stairs and presented myself in front of Tân's room without any of the servants finding out... Under the light bulb was a blue tinsel, and next to a huge mountain-shaped piece of agarwood with thick, swirling aromatic smoke, Tân was leaning against the marble pillar, a violin in hand, playing *Qu'avez vous fait de mon amour*. The melodious tune of the piece brought me back to all the delights of our affair! Upon hearing a sound—I was taking a seat on a bench—Tân turned just a little to look, but didn't put the violin down. His fingers still produced mysterious musical notes of formidable temptation... After completing the piece, he put the instrument down, came to me, and pompously asked,

'So you see, Huyền! Who needs an electric television to enjoy music like Huyền's silly Kim guy, when I'm already an artist? I don't want to torture the ears of my neighbours.'

Finishing that thought, he sat down next to me and kissed my cheek. So Tân hadn't known about that disastrous uncovering! And thus, instead of coming over to inform him of the bad news then cutting ties with him, I suddenly wanted to instigate Tân's love for me.

'Tân... what's the use of us being in love like this? Will it amount to anything?'

'Why are you asking me that? We love for the sake of love. If we have already found happiness in being in love, then we shouldn't be asking whether it'll "amount to anything", because that purpose lies entirely within love's calling already.'

'Do we have any ways to maintain love permanently?'

'We love until we no longer can. When love itself isn't permanent, then who could make it so?'

'That's what you think, but I beg to differ... I want us to love each other forever.'

Tân sprung up, shrugged.

'Oh! So you don't get me yet? What do you want? To divorce your husband? To marry me? How come? That'll never happen! You know for a fact that I detest marriage. If we get married, love will be annihilated! If you want our love to ascend into eternity, keeping it a secret is the only way. That's it. Just think about it, Huyền. Why would Tân love a married woman? Because that love won't cause trouble for me. Meanwhile, that woman will harbour petty resentments from everyday cohabitation as she lives with her husband. This is the very dross of love; she will project it onto her husband, so that she'll show her lover only the purest form of affection! A married woman with a lover will love that lover until the end of her life... Just consider this, Huyền: all roses have thorns. If a man and a woman want to love each other, they must get married, which means the 'thorn' of love is none other than marriage. So in civilised nations, a man's ideal is to have a loyal wife so that he can cheat on her with other lovers, similar to how a woman's ideal is to have an oblivious husband so that she can share the precious essence of love to another lover... The doctrine of husband and wife is one that teaches people to manage each other, frustrate each other, and bicker with each other. In contrast, if we're just casual lovers, then we only have to pamper and spoil each other. A cheating wife or a cuckolded husband—that's the sign of civilisation, when the creator made roses come with thorns, and made love self-destruct with marriage. If we get married officially, we won't love each other with as much passion as this!'

That kind of reasoning, which probably would've been immensely captivating before, now angered me and appeared dishonest to me, if not entirely immoral. I had come to understand—alas, belatedly so—that if we were to consider an idea like that civilised, then civilisation only meant barbarism. Outraged, I snapped back,

'If that's the case, I can't love you anymore!'

Putting his hands into his pants pockets, Tân walked around, pouting.

'Oh, I see, women are really all the same. I'd thought that Huyền was one of the better ones, but now I see clearly that you're just as old-fashioned as those "three subordinations and four virtues"[1] lot!'

'What do you mean "better"? You mean deceiving my husband? Becoming a slave to the guy who tempted me?'

Tân was furious.

---

[1] '三從四德', Confucian moral codes for a woman. The three subordinations refer to obedience to one's father before marriage, one's husband after marriage, and one's son after her husband's death. Four virtues refer to morality, speech, manners, and work ethic considered proper for a woman.

'No! Before you loved me, you already knew what kind of person I was and how my way of thought differs from other people! You loved me of your own volition; I didn't plead, seduce, force or beg you or anything! Just remember and you'll see! When you first loved me, you only thought you were in for a good time and we didn't consider eternity at all. And even an official marriage wouldn't be a foolproof plan.'

Yes, that was the truth! What could I say to that? I could only bury my head in my arms and sob away!

Tân was that type of civilised man, so why on earth did I get involved with him? Seeing my tears, Tân softened and whispered assurances in my ears.

'Anyway, don't cry! Just think for me for a bit! No matter what, I'm still a man of courage and sincerity who dares to speak what I think. If I were lying to you— when I confessed to you and also urged you to leave your husband for me only to abandon you in the end—then I'd be the one at fault here, right? Why didn't you think things through before loving me? Before telling me you understood me? How could I ever marry a woman? You already knew this very well when you loved me, no?'

'But what if this gets found out? What would happen to me?'

'We got our tracks covered so well, how could anyone find out? And I won't be at home for long! I'm leaving for France soon. You just keep on raising your children and serving your husband while thinking of me and loving me in your heart.'

Astonished, I yelped back.

'You? You're going to France again?'

'My dear love, yes! What am I going to do here? This atmosphere is asphyxiating. With just an uneducated, old-fashioned, and barbaric bunch around me! It's still nice, for I have you, but we aren't going to get married, so what's there to worry about? The more we're out of sight, the more we'll yearn for each other!'

I stood up, let out an excruciating sigh, and wailed,

'Well then, I'm done for!'

'What?'

'We've been busted, my dear! I wanted you to save me from my husband's every punishment, but if that's what you plan to do, then from here, I shall also...'

As if still asleep, Tân asked, clueless.

'What? How are we busted? Are you joking or telling the truth? Why's he still treating me so well?'

I recounted everything from beginning to end with great detail. After hearing the whole ordeal, Tân sighed, and then blamed me,

'You are so dumb! Why didn't you deny it? What if it's because he's getting jealous for no reason?'

'Impossible. My husband already knows it all, there's nothing for me to deny!'

'How strange! We cover our tracks so well, how could he have heard about it?'

'That's something you need to explain to me...'

'What if he has a secret spy?'

'Or maybe you have another lover?'

Tân laughed emptily.

'I always have several girls on call! Maybe someone really did tail you and wanted revenge on you, because I love you the most, whereas the other girls are only temporary toys...'

'And me, am I not just another toy?'

Tân shook his head, making excuses.

'My love for you is special, inherently different, and utterly indescribable. I guarantee you that before I die, my last word will be Huyền'

'And what do you think about me now?'

'Well, that's where we have a problem!'

With that, Tân sighed again. He put his hands on his head, thinking. Then he laid on the bench for about half an hour, then sat up and pulled me into a hug as if mourning. Eventually, he let go, opened his safe to grab a diamond ring with two purchase certifications, then slid a second diamond ring off his little finger. Clasping my hands, he said,

'This is the final resort. You take these two rings just in case. Whether you're divorced or still living with him, or returning to your parents, or marrying another person, or having to make ends meet on your own, these two rings will be of use to you in any situation. It pains me that you have no other way. In just about a month, I'm boarding the ship to France! I only have one request for Huyền: that whatever happens, your soul and memories will always have a place for me, that is all. You'll look back and say, "That's the person I loved, and who loved me". Life can separate us, but it can't destroy the love we have for each other!'

Then he placed the two rings in my hands.

That gesture mortified me. Tân simply saw me as a

streetwalker. What an unforgivable gesture! I wasn't an upper-class whore! Those banknotes that the johns handed to prostitutes, or the two diamond rings in my hand—despite their difference in values, they shared the exact same meaning! Tân should've been miserable, sorrowful, wailing his heart out like me, if he truly loved and pitied me... He should've sacrificed his life to save me, conjure up every single way for me to get a divorce, or tell me to join him in committing the last method in the thirty-six stratagems... Was this how Tân loved me? I wanted to get angry, to libel, to slander, to vilify him. Luckily, I reconsidered my situation right away. Right, what duty did Tân have toward me, if I was a mere deplorable woman? I cheated on my husband! I had an affair! If I were to be Tân's wife, who was to say Tân wouldn't be a second cuckolded husband? One could love many things, but an unfaithful person was where one drew the line. If I wanted to blame someone, I had myself to blame first!

I looked at Tân's face... an indifferent, incompre -hensible face with too little emotion.

Thus, I stood up resolutely, ripped apart the receipts and threw them at Tân's face, and hurled the two diamond rings away before him!

Before he could say anything, I had already stormed

out of the room with the resentful attitude of an indignant woman. He called for me two, three times, but I thought if I turned around, I'd lose my value once again. I came home. And the fact that I rejected the two rings worth thousands of silvers was another cause for the regret and remorse I felt when I involved myself in the darker side later on.

I never met Tân again. Neither did he have the guts to show his face to his friend, one who had put too much trust in friendship in this era where individualism reigned supreme.

And then, one day, the owners of stallion barns, the waiters at grand hotels, the photographers, the frequent patrons of dance clubs and of tailor shops for modern clothes—they no longer spoke of the most refined, dashing, and chivalrous young master in all of Hà Nội, the one with the sedan of twelve horsepower that, even when on street roads, accelerated so rapidly like aeroplanes from overseas!

And Huyền, Mrs. Adminstrateur Kim, the belle of the capital, was no longer seen at gatherings of the upper-class anymore.

In those three to four months, I lived a most resigned life in the kitchen corner, without a single idea of equality or liberation. I did not even think of vain extravagance next to an inscrutable husband, who couldn't even bother to speak a word of intimacy to me. Instead, he treated me like a stranger and always spent the night out. With nothing to do but eat and lie around, I'd morphed into the obedient Japanese woman. Sometimes, I'd put my oil lamp on low light, waiting for my esteemed husband until four in the morning. When he came back, he'd pound on the door, enter, drink the cup of water I prepared, wash his face with the bucket of water I carried, throw his hat and jacket onto the bed for me to clean up, then get on the bed and sleep, without a single order or word of gratitude. He didn't even bother reproaching me when I made a mistake. That policy of expressing disdain through silence was thousands of times more cruel than all scolding and beating combined. But what could I do? I still had to endure it without breathing a word to anyone. As the old servants had all been fired, the new driver and nanny had nothing but high praise for me, saying that my husband was the most fortunate man to have a wife who was so subservient. In front of my husband, they dared not raise their voice. When my husband was home, an air of fear and reverence filled the house. I slept on a separate bed, and dined with the nanny and driver. They didn't find it strange, having familiarised themselves with every habit of this new domestic landscape.

Throughout this time, every guest of his or every guest

of mine was a saviour, a benefactor for me, even though it was just for a short while... Whenever the house received a new guest, my husband would at least be obliged to speak to me in a few affectionate and intimate words, to show that we still treated each other well as husband and wife. Those special occasions thrilled me and gave me the illusion that that irreparable incident had never happened in our domestic lives. But the more ecstatic I felt, the more pain I suffered. Because once the guests took their leave, once the table was left with only an empty betel bowl and some cups lined with leftover tea, my esteemed husband's apathetic face was enough to make me feel as if the entire house had been besieged by winter. As for those sweet words he spoke to me earlier, oh dear! They were anything but those of a priest consoling prisoners on death row before they stepped out onto the execution site with the headsman.

It would've been redundant to say this was a life not worth living anymore.

I was living the life of a concubine imprisoned in a cold palace, even though I was always the closest to the king. My position was even more humiliating than that of a prisoner—at least a prisoner, no matter how severe their crime and how long their sentence, could still harbour a slight hope for amnesty.

One day, when I paid a visit to my parents' home, I suddenly felt the entire household behaving curtly around me. My father glanced at me then shrugged once, disappointed, which was to be expected. But my mother didn't even ask after me, which surprised me greatly! I believed that I was truly considered an absolute stranger, if not entirely worthless scum. I stood up, then sat down, drank an insipid cup of tea, chewed on a betel that tasted too bland in my mouth, spoke words that felt strangely disagreeable, acted in gestures that felt strangely awkward, in the home of my birth parents. This was where I grew up, yet I was now seen as a passer-by. I guessed my husband must've told my side of the family about my irredeemable sin.

As I was about to take my leave out of embarrassment, one of my sisters called me down to the kitchen and asked me under her breath.

'How have you been treating him recently that he's been acting so heartless to us?'

Quickly I asked.

'Well, what did my husband tell you?'

My sister replied.

'If I knew, I wouldn't have asked you!'

Inside, I felt a bit of relief: my husband wasn't so cruel as to cut off my last holy line of communication with the most precious people in my life. Then I made up an answer.

'I... I haven't done anything.'

My words were immediately corrected by my tears! No matter how hard I tried to suppress them, I still couldn't help but feel resentful; the hiccups were uncontainable and unstoppable. My sister, both in shock and out of pity, gaped at me, shook my shoulders, trying to get the entire story out of me, but I only stuttered.

'Oh dear! My sister!... You have no idea about the bitter pains... the misery... that I'm going through! Right now... but it doesn't matter—one day, soon enough, you'll know everything.'

I hurriedly took my leave like an escapee. Passing by my mother, I gave her only a quick goodbye, having no courage to look into the face of a mother who had nothing but love for me. When I brushed the curtain aside to step out, I didn't turn back. I knew my mother was watching me with the petrified heart only a kind mother was capable of.

That was the last time!

From then on, never... ever did I see my parents' face again!

That day, after coming home, an urge to kill myself suddenly overtook me! Surely, when a person had committed the acts that I did, then that person wouldn't deserve to live, right? My family didn't have the full details on anything, and yet they behaved so coldly towards me. If my husband came forward with the truth, and even went so far as to humiliate his wife's parents, then my father's shame would snowball to unbearable degrees; my family's disdain towards me would escalate to terrifying heights! Recognising that I was truly all by myself on this earth, I was further convinced that this life was unliveable. Then... there was only one way, the most effective and effortless method for those fed up with life. Consequently, that night, I immediately went to buy three bottles of sleeping pills.

And yet I didn't end my life. Technically speaking, I hadn't ended my life. From deep inside me, I still felt something akin to a sliver of hope, even though whenever I tried to reason it out, I found that hope was not worth keeping anymore. Why was it so? I couldn't understand that myself. I just knew that for days on end, whenever I wanted to urge myself to make a choice, I granted myself another deadline. 'If death was the only way out, then why the rush? You can die anytime, no?'

I still tried to tell myself that. Truthfully speaking, it was cowardice: the desire to live and the fear of dying was so natural to human instinct. Thanks to this, humankind still existed and only a precious few dared to die. All in spite of the fact that everyone who had ever lived had undergone painful experiences, so painful that they wanted death as a way out of this curse human world.

I tried my best to use the very last drop of my energy to hope that perhaps my husband would reconsider and forgive me... During that time, every order from my husband was a special privilege, and a half-baked and irritated reprimand, too, had the power of a promise of amnesty!

In the midst of that tortuous period of half-living, half-dying, I saw the face of my old lover one day in the newspaper. There was a picture with a caption, 'A beauty pageant in Sài Gòn Market', where I saw Tân, yes, actually Tân, sitting in the front row in the shaded area, among the judges and in front of many beautiful women posing and flexing their bodies. My blood had just enough time to make one run through my veins! I was seething and nearing madness, even though I already knew I should've calmed down. I couldn't forgive Tân for his crime of causing so many catastrophes to befall me, then abandoning me in hell to take his sweet time ascending to every heavenly scene on earth!... It turned out that while I was struggling this much, Tân was enjoying himself that much! I ripped the entire newspaper apart.

The day after, I came to look for Hội. I asked for news about Tân in the name of my husband.

'Dear, my husband complained that ever since sir Tân went to Sài Gòn, he's only sent out one letter. My husband sent in several and hasn't heard back from him.'

Hội answered me with a question.

'How could that be?'

'That's why my husband told me to come here and ask you whether sir Tân has boarded the ship to France.'

Hội answered with conviction.

'He's going to be in Sài Gòn for at least three more months before leaving for France.'

'Why's he staying there for so long?'

'He's waiting for a friend, the son of some chef de province, to wrap up some private business. Then they'll leave together.'

'Is that confirmed?'

'Absolutely! The letter he sent out to me the other day said so!'

I asked about Tân's current address, then took my leave.

Upon returning home, I felt that I had to look for Tân

by all means, even if I had to climb the highest mountain and sail the seven seas... This hellish environment, really, was enough reason for me to break out and run away.

Why did I want to look for Tân?

At the time, I didn't answer myself right away. Perhaps I only planned to find Tân with the sole purpose of killing him to satisfy myself, that was all. Was I lying to myself at that time? Who knows!

But if someone asked me—if only someone would ask me—whether I felt remorse, then I'd assert with no hesitation: I was already deeply remorseful. Life and the human heart, both were such complicated matters!

For days, I was still reluctant, and neither did I have the courage to think it through. I wanted to postpone it by overthinking the matter, or to rationalise it so that it made moral sense, because I feared that, once I could see through the ways of life, I'd never be able to make up my mind. I only knew that back then, I resented Tân with my entire being to the point that if we were to meet, I might as well have pulled out a dagger and plunged it straight into his heart without batting an eye. I didn't know that resentment meant that there was still love. If we were to meet and Tân not only stopped acting so curtly but also agreed to let me accompany him wherever I wanted, to stay with him wherever I wished, would I have cultivated enough hatred to kill that traitor, to avenge my thoroughly wrecked life? I couldn't bring myself to even think about that problem.

Then, one day, I left my husband a letter that read as follows.

> *'My dear,*
>
> *I am writing to request your permission for my absence from the household for a short period of time. Where I am heading and for what purpose, you shall learn of it sooner or later. I hope that upon my return, I will have made up for my mistakes of the past. If I do not return, then you should consider me dead.*
>
> *Oh dear, I wanted to take this opportunity to confide in you many things, yet I fear you will shrug your shoulders and frown again... And so I have no choice but to wait for the day of my return, when I can speak to you as you willingly listen, and I hope that my temporary departure from the household will not bother you too much.*
>
> *Signed,*
>
> *Your miserable wife'*

Two days later, at noon, in a fourth-class cabin of a

train headed south, there was a young woman with the looks of a recently recovered beauty, shivering in an overcoat. She only had one small suitcase as her luggage. Amidst other passengers who were travelling in groups, she was by herself, huddled into a corner to hide her face. She waited for the conductor with the red flag to blow on his whistle and usher the passengers in, all the while terrified of stumbling across a familiar face...

That young woman was this Huyền.

I had sold my jewellery and taken another risk in life. And, oddly enough, once the train began to move, I felt no sense of hesitation or regret in my conscience! This journey, back when I was still planning it, gave me a great deal of concern, but it had now become an unexpected escape. Only then did I know I had the spirit of most streetwalkers! To normal people, perhaps they considered that their individual ideology must've been the only one to exist, never to change—but to people of the street, ideologies manifested in millions of ways depending on how much they wanted to approve or disapprove of others. For the souls of the streets, they would still lie to others with virtuous ideas, even regarding perverse matters. Thus, when I intended to look for Tân, I only focused on how to exact revenge and erase the humiliation I suffered at the hands of my husband by killing Tân. At this point, the idea of killing my former lover stopped appearing so enticingly novel! It'd depend on whether I'd be treated well or poorly. Because only then did I remember that if we violated someone's right to life, we'd be thrown into jail and lose our heads, instead of achieving freedom for ourselves! ...Murder! As if that was as easy as killing a mosquito!

Certainly, a travelling student on this train would imagine arriving in a whole new world. It would be abundant with promises of a life filled to the brim with risks that could send us to ecstasy, or with fortunes that would push us into the thorny pits of hell. Both of these foreshadowed a land of the unforeseeable, the unexpected, the incomprehensibility of future ups and downs, which were the spices that flavoured our upcoming adventure. The more the journey unsettled us, the more it urged us to forge forward with vigour. I, too, shared that kind of attitude. And so as I sat on the train, I didn't bother thinking about rationalising anything, leaving myself entirely to my instincts. I floated away with the chuggity-chug cadence of the train against the metal rail. I barely had time to sketch a vague agenda of what to do when I met that suspicious man who was my treacherous lover. I'd detail to Tân how my husband had treated me and elaborate on the hellish nature of that mental punishment, in order to have him take part of the responsibility... And if Tân reacted badly by cutting ties with me, like an appendix to be removed despite the pain, then I'd come up with a way to handle it thoroughly. Though I hadn't thought of how, I'd ensure that this woman would do everything in her power to make the modern playboy suffer. He'd be humiliated, paralysed, unable to lift his head, so that it'd be deserving of my journey and worthy of a 'messy' quarrel. I could act as the Grim Reaper tailing a patient on the operating table, if that person had the gall to cut things off... I must do it, even though I was merely entertaining such thoughts. But even so, wasn't that enough? Should a woman's life be like mine, that is, consisting of one risk after another from childhood to adulthood—then what good would come of the cautious women? The only thing worth telling was that I was still laying low after daring to escape my husband's hell, and that was all you should know. During that time of punishment, every minute felt as long as a year, every year as long as a century, so my running away from home was very much worth it. Yes, I took a risk! Now that I'd risked it, what else could I need!

Yet life still had many things in store for us to desire. That was truly lamentable, despite us having risked it!

Once I arrived at Sài Gòn and found Tân's address, I learned that he had just left on a trip to Angkor Wat and Angkor Thom.

They said Tân would be away for a whole week, and whereas I should've stayed in Sài Gòn to save money, impatience got the better half of me and so I went to Angkor as well. Like finding a needle in a haystack, I dragged myself through endless houses to search for Tân, sparing no mental energy to notice the unimaginably magnificent architecture of our old neighbouring nation Cambodia. When I finally found where he had been staying in Angkor, I was stupefied to find out that he had just returned to Phnom Penh. When it rained, it poured; when I went back to Phnom Penh, the hotel owner told me Tân had already set foot in Sài Gòn. When I reached Sài Gòn, the money I had left could only afford me two more meals!

Did Tân find out about this beforehand to run away from me? Just asking myself that question was enough to wreck me as I couldn't bring myself to believe it. But it seemed like there was no end to reaping what one sowed, for once I found Tân's accommodation in Sài Gòn, I learned that my lover had gone to Bangkok with his friend to travel the seas and mountains... At that point, my conviction had reached its breaking point. While I was determined to climb mountains and sail across seas, an issue arose: I had no money. I was devastated when I went to the Police Department of Sài Gòn and was told that if I couldn't make a deposit of two hundred silvers, I had no shot at crossing the border to the capital of Siam.

That was it! What use was love, and what worth was even resentment or revenge, if we couldn't resolve the problem of how to feed ourselves the day after? Now that I'd risked it, what else could I need? It was only an effective idea when I stepped foot onto that train. As always, people only knew they messed up once it was too late.

And so, the pressing matter was no longer about deciding whether to wait for Tân's return, or myself returning to... that place where I must return. It was a matter of how to buy tomorrow's meals, how to pay rent, how to address the sharp glances riddled with suspicion from the hotel owners, and the waiters' whispers behind closed doors, so certain that I was a streetwalker abandoned in a foreign land, all by myself...

Here was a young woman who was relatively good-looking but had no money; she had been knocked down enough and was now lost in an unknown land. How would she be treated by men? Would they take pity? Let me tell you how they actually decided to shove that woman into the mud... Because they were waiting to ask me directly: 'Hey, where the hell did you come from? Are you chasing a man or were you chased out by your husband? Or are you a virgin itching to reveal your true nature, so you left home to pursue a man? This woman doesn't look like she is of decency, because if she really is, then well, whyever would she be?'. These were the facts of the matter. Even an undeniably, inviolably good person, who accidentally fell into circumstances such as mine, would struggle to maintain their morals, let alone a true corrupt woman who had never learned to treasure what was most important her entire life.

'Hey ya, don't worry too much about wasting yer money, yeah? Try talkin' and hangin' out with one of our patrons fer a night, and we on top of the food chain again!'

Not once did I forget those precious eye-opening words from the hotel owner, who was also the number one pimp in my life as an escort.

The following day, unable to stay still or come up with any plausible plan, I acquiesced to 'talking' for a night with one of the johns who was from Bạc Liêu. Then, after seeing the pile of banknotes under the pillow, I burst into tears, sobbing like a motherless orphan living with an evil stepmother who had accidentally broken the most precious vase in the house.

But that was barely enough! Once I could afford today's meals, I had to think about what to do for tomorrow's meals. If I had money to spare after food, I had to calculate the cost of returning to the North. After I had enough for the train, I changed my mind again, wanting to linger around to wait for Tân to return to Sài Gòn, or even to find Tân all the way in Bangkok! When I ran out of patience and hope of meeting my former lover and decided to come back, I found out that the money I had made was also gone! As I kept hesitating, unsure of what decision to make, I'd already spent exactly one month in the South before I even knew it.

The first time I sold myself to a john didn't go smoothly. Any person on earth, no matter how debauched and cowardly, still had at least some pride in them, like a little nagging from their conscience. And so I had to tell myself and console myself: 'If I don't risk it, then what other ways do I have?... Besides, I'm not that pure to begin with, so even if I get a bit dirtier, it'll be "harmless". When we walk on a muddy road, we'll try to find dry patches of land so as not to dirty our new shoes... But what if we're unlucky and step on mud again and again? What's the point of keeping them clean now? Might as well close our eyes and push forward so that we can get over it soon. Furthermore, we can decide to give in to fate only this one time...' Woe is me, for I had to give in for a second time even after reminding myself with the exact same words. And then on the third time... it was over!

Long gone was my shame, my pride, my conscience

tugging at me! Just keep practising, and soon you'll become perfect at the craft...

When I knew for certain that Tân had boarded the ship to France from Bangkok, I finally made my return to the North. When I parted ways with Sài Gòn, I genuinely didn't feel any regret at all, because I had no intention of continuing this courtesan profession. I still wanted to turn my life around.

But once I arrived at Hà Nội, some kind of frightening force threatened me to the point where I couldn't gather enough courage to return to my husband or my parents, even though I constantly told myself: if I dared to take the risk and left, then I might as well dare to take the risk and return. Yet, how could I face them? How could I speak to them? I could never understand the wacky, self-conflicting character of a woman who had the guts to sell herself to an unknown john but couldn't for the life of her have enough courage to entertain the thought of coming back and facing her beloveds, even if it meant just taking a bet on her dignity for one last time.

And thus, although I should've taken a different path, I took a turn onto this route, came to that madame, the bulky boss who talked to you heartily the other night.

From then until now, this tumultuous, fleeting life of a streetwalker... has had its ups and downs. There were moments of ecstasy so great that they turned into tears, and of sorrow so profound they came out as laughter. I could only console myself with filthy pleasures and block out every thought about the future. If I were to consciously think about my life, I realised that the way the Heavens dealt with every act of careful preservation and every visionary reconstruction of mankind was utterly sterile!

In the End

Worn out, Huyền set the notebook on the pillow, sat up with great difficulty, then poured herself some water...

Both bottles of beer were now empty. The cups were lined with some yellow residue, the shells of pumpkin seeds were scattered all over the pillows and mattress, the peanut oil lamp wearily mustered the most feeble light—such signs indicated that it was time to conclude this carouse, even though I wasn't sure if the story ended there... Thoughts and feelings shoved themselves against my senses like oceanic white caps crashing disappointingly against the rock mounds amidst a powerful gale, and so I remained lying down in silence to taste that cacophony of the mind. I closed my eyes and allowed my thoughts to run wild...

But then Quý suddenly asked.

'Is that all, dear? Is that where it ends?'

Huyền replied.

'I want to write more, but it's hard to find the time...'

Then she lay down again, crossing her arm across her forehead with a concerning, fatigued expression. I sat up, worried.

'That's all we have, but that's already enough!'

Huyền looked at me with a gleeful twinkle in her eyes.

I took the notebook, flipped through it again and again as if I were examining a book of magnificent paintings, even though my eyes only saw a riddle of hardly legible handwriting in pencil. Huyền's life, almost her entire life, was summarised in that flimsy file. No matter what, I still thought of Huyền as loveable, in the sense that she was smarter than the majority—if not all—of streetwalkers. And thanks to that notebook, perhaps what Huyền considered useless wouldn't be so useless to other women. Contemplating how to put these notes to good use, I took a most satisfying inhale from the pipe tobacco, then solemnly said.

'Huyền, dear Huyền, I'd like to thank you...'

She turned to me, filled with innocent surprise, and asked,

'Huh? Why are you thanking me?'

I felt a sudden sense of urgency.

'Thank you for these precious notes that you gave us to read, for the stories you gladly recounted, for taking the time to elaborate for us when we didn't fully understand what we'd read, and especially for the rare honesty that you've graciously allowed us to indulge in!'

Huyền let out a brisk laugh and spoke tenderly.

'What's there to be thankful for? You're clearly making this up to be so sentimental... It goes without saying: because I wanted to use my experience for good, I put in the effort to write down my entire life. Once I have it written down, it's not for me to keep or for my children and grandchildren to worship on the altar, if I ever get to have a husband and children, that is... Then I should be the one to thank you, shouldn't I? All those tasteless johns and I still got to meet you like this; isn't that the same as entering a market and coincidentally stumbling across your old friend...'

'Well, we indeed are each other's old friends, aren't we?'

'Surely! That was just my figure of speech.'

'Then let me take home this precious memoir right away...'

'Oh no, I'll finish it first then ask for your help later.'

After some pondering, I was determined.

'No need, this is already way more than enough.'

Not following me, Huyền looked at me again with her big, passionate eyes.

'Because if you were to write more, it'd perhaps be redundant.'

Still not following, Huyền asked again,

'But I haven't finished writing about the part of my life after I got into this business of debauchery up until now?'

I had no choice but to explain to her in detail, despite my terror that I'd say something out of line.

'As far as the public is concerned, the life of someone like you—someone who suddenly fell out of stability and into difficult circumstances—that's the only part they'll pay attention to. Why would a child of a proper and decent family, and a noble one at that, turn out so lost to the point of... debauchery, the public only cares about the reasons leading up to it... On the other hand, a book describing a life of debauchery, from the moment you began that life, seems of little use to anyone. That's why I told you there's no need to write more.'

I'd perhaps alleviated Huyền of a burden on her shoulders. Happiness was painted on her face with such vibrancy. She sat up straight again, energetic, and poured tea for us as well. When we didn't have enough cups, she yelled for the waiter incessantly. Finally, she told me,

'Then I get it. Before, I thought I had to take even more notes, which was such a hassle for me, as I didn't know when the book would be over... Alright, then— please take it home.'

Even though I didn't need to take it right away, I still did. I set the notebook next to me, to signal to myself that I had ownership over that object. Huyền spoke again.

'You can make adjustments, add things, leave things out, arrange it somehow to make it comprehensible, and just go ahead and publish it... That's the only thing I ask of you.'

'You don't need to tell me twice. And besides, there aren't many edits to be made...'

Huyền looked for some oil then rubbed her hands together.

'Great, if it weren't for your guidance, I would've thought I wasn't done with such an important task! Ah, let me go downstairs and get the waiter to pour us more water... Damn, I'm so thirsty!'

Quý the teacher took the notebook, gave it a good look, then commented.

'A stack of paper... a whole life... endless horrifying truths...'

Worried that my dearest friend would do something that was worth calling the cops on, I jerked the notebook away from him. Luckily, Quý kept his mouth shut instantly. With hands on her hips, Huyền pouted and criticised herself.

'Endless wicked, horrifying, nauseating truths...'

Despite knowing that Huyền wasn't trying to take a jab at anyone, I still added,

'If this piece were to bring about any value, then that would be because it describes those very truths, those very evils...'

Huyền stood there for a while, then headed downstairs.

The clock chimed four times on this day of drizzle and wind as the night was coming to a close. Life was cracking open yet another daybreak.

Only now did my friend express his honest nature to me. He shook his head at me.

'For three nights straight, we went from beer to

opium, and as soon as we finished drinking we craved the smoke to prevent ourselves from getting drunk. When we sobered up we wanted to smoke again to stay up and listen, and after smoking we needed drinks to help with the thirst in our throats... No offence, but should life be as cyclical as that endless loop? Just to hear why a woman has become corrupt? If a thousand women have stories to share, you'll have to count me out! No more, no more— I'll leave tomorrow.'

Suddenly I felt a sense of antagonism toward my friend, thinking that this man really got to have his cake and eat it too! I could've absolutely cut ties with him, if I didn't give it a second thought. Wasn't my friend completely head over heels the first time he saw Huyền? Wasn't I the nonchalant one when we faced his problems in love? Wasn't I worried sick that perhaps Quý would have lingering feelings and things would get extremely messy, because I might be the one responsible for wrecking another person's home? Now that Quý could bring himself to say such words, I could truly rest assured that nothing would happen to my friend later on. I sighed, my body infinitely lighter. Then I was surprised once more, wondering why Quý was so quick to change his mind. After listening to an extended confession—even an elaborate repentance—from the very beauty with whom he was once infatuated, Quý not only did not spare any tears of pity, but his love for her ran so low that he was cold-blooded and indifferently brutal. Thus, I asked him,

'Are you not... in love with your Muse anymore?'

Calmly, Quý shook his head.

'Why did you cry so strangely the other night, then?'

Quý answered with a question.

'Right, why was I acting so effeminate then, when now my heart is sobbing no more, to the point of such dispassion?'

Seeing my lack of response, my friend, after some time, added,

'But... in the end... for a child of a decent family to end up like that, it'd be hard to take pity on her! Too promiscuous, too corrupt—who would've thought?'

I remained silent. My friend had turned into a mediocre man who did not share the same worldview as me. Even if there were a comprehensive philosophy, my friend would probably not get it. Besides... What was the point? Life wasn't at all perfect, but with that mediocre brain, wouldn't that ease the world of so many 'messy' matters? And suddenly I was convinced that the *majority* of us men were on the same level of emotional capacity as my friend, if I weren't to go so far as to speculate that all men were at that threshold: obediently and peacefully mediocre. That was a type of luck, too!

But out of nowhere, my friend's tone shifted, his diction changed as he asked me seriously,

'Oh crap! You're going to publish this as it is?'

'There's not much to edit.'

'You're keeping those passages depicting... uncensored descriptions of carnal matters?'

Surprised, I asked him,

'Why not?'

'Are you serious?'

My surprise had now turned into frustration. Alright, I really had to spell it out for my friend at this rate! So I told him.

'Good grief! It's because this entire text is about carnal matters! You want me to edit or even omit passages that retell the truth? Good grief; the corrupt woman is that very truth, even if it takes the form of evil truths! The public doesn't know or simply sweeps those evils under the rug, purposefully acting stupid and thereby harming countless other people just from turning a blind eye. Of course I have to make it so they won't turn a blind eye anymore. We're surrounded by evil and mischief, but once many people come to know about it, surely there'll be ways to prevent, alleviate, and repair it! Forcing me not to talk about the debauchery of carnal pleasures? Why don't you find a way to force people not to be corrupt! Forcing me to leave out passages that accurately depict the evil and filthy truths in this text? Then why don't you force Huyền to stop being corrupt, and force this society to stop having tens of thousands of whores like Huyền, wouldn't that be simpler?'

'Then aren't you afraid that the hypocrites will attack you?'

'With that malicious kind, it's best to stay disdainfully silent. Besides, we're lucky to be in the era of science now. People are putting in the effort to pay attention, investigate, and research. In that sense, the fate of the hypocrites or those who choose the immoral route seem rather bleak.'

'However, we should take precautions... We shouldn't forget that Kiều[1] was once condemned as a sexually provocative book.'

'Stop telling people to keep being cowards, because

---

[1] Referring to Thúy Kiều, the protagonist of Nguyễn Du's *The Tale of Kiều*, who was the beautiful and virtuous daughter of a fallen noble family. She sold herself into prostitution to save her father.

even without you, people have been cowards long enough! I understand what I'm doing, so outsiders should rest assured. Once a nation is invaded and forced to bring out the military, as drafted men we only have two ways out: one is to kill the enemy, the other is to be killed by the enemy. How do you expect to advise a soldier not to kill the enemy or to prevent himself from getting killed? It'd be better to make him stay at home, then!'

I still had more to say, so much more to say, but outside, Huyền was already making her way up. She had in her hand a kettle of boiling water, which tainted her entire hand, as white as snow. She noticed that I had put my jacket on and her face darkened...

'Are you leaving already? Please stay a while longer!'

I consoled her.

'You look exhausted, so we want you to rest...'

Then she told us something we never expected.

'I couldn't care less about exhaustion, even if we had to stay up for three days straight, as long as we've managed to resolve the anxiety that's been plaguing our life!'

Before I knew it, the clock chimed five times again.

After my friend finished his cup of tea, I saw that his face had evidently become withered and tarnished. I suddenly feared for myself as well. I knew for sure that I shouldn't keep wallowing in pity and linger here for much longer, so I held both of Huyền's hands.

'Once again, I would like to thank you sincerely.'

Lady Kiều allowed me a glimpse at her pearly white teeth once more and whispered to me,

'Please... let me share this with you.'

Commendably quick-witted, Quý immediately drifted toward the window with his back to us, acting as if he was occupied with the grey landscape of early morning. And, instead of saying anything, Huyền only wrapped her arms around my neck and bid me goodbye with a kiss that I thought was out of love, that made me think perhaps I was... a lady's man!

Then Huyền shook Quý's hands, dignified.

Three hours later, on that very same day, my friend returned to the highlands. When we parted ways, I could only express my gratitude to him with a firm handshake, thanking him for crying in a slightly embarrassing way, which allowed me to offer to the nation this precious docu-novel.

***

Dear Huyền!

Your life novel—here it is, right here.

Has it achieved its purpose and fulfilled our wishes? I mean to say—has it satisfied your hopes that your total sincerity and my efforts would at least amount to something of some use? Who could tell if Huyền's murky body made clear again[1] was enough for life to forgive her sins, even though life lacked no contradictions where the water was murky while the dust was clear[2]!

Thanks to you, I've had the good fortune to understand why us humans are evil, why we're filthy, and most importantly, why we're suffering. It's also thanks to you that I got to learn about the crucial lessons of life, that the evil and the unease which we think are unique only to us are also the same evil and the unease of another person, if not of many other people. You've lived a filthy life plagued with an unfortunate turn of events, and it is your wish that by publishing your catastrophic life to the world, you're doing a considerably kind thing with your entire life... While that's very

---

[1] References to line 3183 of *The Tale of Kiều* (Nguyễn Du, translated by Nguyễn Bình, Major Books, 2025).

[2] References to line 879 of *The Tale of Kiều* (Nguyễn Du, translated by Nguyễn Bình, Major Books, 2025).

greedy of you to wish for some kind of redemption, my own wish when I got involved in this matter is no different.

But... where are you now, Huyền? What have you become? Are you still in the depths of hell on earth, or have you ascended to a life of riches?

If we're not careful, we might end up completely misunderstanding each other...

Regardless of what happens, we surely cannot forget this: you're a streetwalker, while I'm a one-night stand... Especially not when we've made our vow. I mustn't care about your future, and you'll make sure to prevent yourself from causing trouble to the unperturbed family of this poor student. And I can never forget everything you told me! '*I found the way the Heavens dealt with every act of careful preservation and every visionary reconstruction of mankind utterly sterile... That's why, in the future, even if I were riding in a private sedan or pushing an ox cart; having a founding father kneel at my feet or being beaten and berated by several husbands from the brothel; dying on an eight pole palanquin accompanied by many Legion of Honour recipients or dying a damning death in charity hospitals, then I'll take it. Who would waste their time worrying about a yellowed leaf falling off in an entire forest of greenery!'* That's right, whether you're basking in luxury or wallowing in misery, I, as promised, will pay it no mind.

But still, Huyền, do you remember that day we met for the last time? We didn't expect it to be the last time, because we never said it would be our last time. The Saturday two weeks after, I came back to where we met, and was unexpectedly told: 'She eventually came back and waited for you for a long time!... We're not sure where she's gone now, and no one knows where to look for her.' Oh Huyền, I couldn't describe to you how sorrowful I felt upon hearing this. Even though I said I wouldn't care, I also feared that I made a mistake; how can I meet you when I want to apologise now? And so I have to take a risk with this remaining passage to finish what I want to say to Huyền, to answer a doubt that you brought up several times. No, I do not look down on you! If I haven't found ways to defend you, then that was because I wanted to keep a neutral stance so that the public could comment however they wanted... Do you understand, my dear Huyền? Because if that's the case, then you can hand this piece of your life to your lover or your jealous husband who wants to trace your sins all the way to the start, and say: 'Here—as for why I ended up this way, the reasons are all here... this is my life, though the names of characters and streets have been changed.'

If this story isn't useful to many, then just think that it's not absolutely useless in the sense that it's helped you personally in that aspect.

Finally, I want to make sure: did I make any mistakes or misunderstand anything, or did I 'go against' Huyền in any detail here? If you're happy with how this turns out, write to me.

And, because you'll get angry at me, I won't thank you again in this text.

October, 1936.

Inquiry to Mr. Thái Phỉ, owner of Literary News journal, with regards to the article *On Lewd Literature*

In issue 25 of *Literary News journal* recently, you sent out a warning to realist writers on the matter of lewd literature.

I am writing my response to you through this letter not because I admit to my writing being dirty, but because I am one of those writers of realism. If your warning was written in a way that suited the curvature of my ear canals, I certainly would have dropped my pen in surrender to your wishes; I am one of those who knows how to restore moral goodness, yet I am still in dire need for others to point out my own shortcomings. Yes, who dares to be so completely conceited as to never do anything bad?

Yet damningly, your warning not only horrified me, but also made me disappointed. Don't be petulant; I'm horrified simply because I couldn't understand how a person who works for literature such as you could have such round

-about and murky reasonings. And my disappointment comes from how an owner of a literary company could hold such blurry, dusky, chaotic conceptions of literature such as you—that truly is a disgrace, and, what's more, a crime of blasphemy towards literature.

Here, let me quote the sentences you had written just to see whether I'm right or wrong.

In the opening, you had said:

'But if only these old folks would know how to relish such literature of the lewd in French literature—then they will know that to the French, despite the lewdness, literature remains literature.

It's not that literature must always be truthfully elegant. When describing anything—it could be atrocious or filthy—if it attains the completeness of art, then that is also literature.'

I would like to thank you, yes, thank you very much— did you hear me clearly enough? But what exactly does it mean to attain the completeness of art? You haven't explained it directly, meaning you denounce the things that you consider to be incomplete

'They (the four realist writers) see that society favours the lewd, so they either try to stuff lewdness into any writings of theirs, or intentionally describe the lewd in a way that is too provocative on the principle of realism. In doing so, they mince it into unsightliness. They try too hard to thrill the readers' senses rather than think about art.'

After letting the readers understand the context, from here on, I would like to quote you verbatim to elucidate the lewd. Lewdness by itself is not filth if it is not disorderly. The lewdness that exists between a husband and a wife, for example, is akin to the normalcy of eating; it is not polluted or dirty, but is considered to be noble and gracious. Still, people don't need to describe that, for it would be pornographic. However, there are the kinds of lewd that deserve to be called filth, such as rape, adultery, incest—meaning the lewdness that belongs to men and women who are not linked by marriage. The realist writer has the right and duty to describe such things, bearing in mind that they are the kinds of lewd that are polluted and dirty. To realistically describe such an event in all its filthy, degrading glory is to reach the completeness of art—or how else would you, Mr. Thái Phỉ, like to have it?

But here Mr. Thái Phỉ continues to claim:

'Because these people describe everything with such nakedness, such raw inelegance, anyone who knows how to read would find it repulsive. They want to lay bare reality in all its glory, whilst forgetting that when you speak of reality so nakedly, people would come to fear it instead of enjoying it.'

Oh, how strange it is what you speak of! You want to force the realist writers to see such acts as noble, graceful, and easily befitting morality, so that they can copy those dirty things in the stories? All while describing the filthy, pornographic realities to make readers fall in love? You have the right to dislike our rawness, but you don't have the right to force us to sexually excite the readers!

But your waves of wild stupidity lose sight of the shore with your reasonings I mentioned above. Unbearably, you dare to advise us with this: 'It is due to such explicitness that I have to pen this article, for I hope that the artists who write lewd literature will rein in their momentum before it's too late. Don't leave it until the public starts to uproar in indignation.'

Indignation? That is all we wish for!

But that indignation—that completeness of art—is what the public uses to counter the dirtiness and the mistakes in morality that we describe in the stories. And such indignation is very terrifying, but they do not direct it towards the storyteller like how Mr. Thái Phỉ does.

Esteemed sirs, if I tattle to you that there is someone who commits such atrocious, filthy, adulterous and disgusting acts like this and that someone is amongst your friends or your children…then will you feel indignant towards men, the person who simply denounces such atrocities? If, instead of thanking me, you are filled with indignation like what Mr Thái Phỉ claims, then dear me! I have no need to concern myself with such meaningless indignation?!

But why did Mr. Thái Phỉ decide to pen this meandering, childish warning? Why Mr. Thái Phỉ?

Maybe it's actually on you, in accordance with what you have confessed in On Lewd Literature: 'No, I am no saint, I am only human, but in each human being there exists a beast. If we don't try to rein it in carefully and let it awaken, then it will do evil immediately!'

Damn! You speak as if you are sick, as if you are haunted by an awful obsession (*hantise*) that is extremely dangerous for fine customs and traditions. You are an abnormality (*anormal*) that very much deserves an examination by Dr. Magnus Hirchleld, who is researching the filthy lewdness of abnormal people for his book. Your sickness—that obsession—has led you to lose all reason to the point where you lose all joy (*resie*) when you read a passage that describes raw, filthy disgustingness. You would rather have the author write a shiny and sleek kind of literature for your enjoyment, only then for you to become disgusted, and even indignant. Yet you will still be unable to contain the beast inside of you—that is what is truly unreasonable—to the point where you will suffer under the claws of that beast!

For the last time, I implore you to continue retching, feeling nauseated and disgusted when you read any passage that describes a filthy, obscene scene. Endeavour to contain the beast inside of you. Stop desiring anything, and stop forcing anyone to use elegant, half-censored prose when they describe a dirty scene. In a way that you won't feel any embarrassment when reading it out loud but instead, you should find it totally interesting, literary, and joyful; you should want to hum it out loud; you should want to re-read it in order to carefully consider the lewd!

I implore you to go cure yourself of that sickness first, only then shall we talk literature.

Respectfully,

Vũ Trọng Phụng
Hanoi Journal, no. 38, 23rd September 1936

A few notes on this translation of Making a Whore, from the publisher

The language in *Làm Đĩ* serves as a snapshot of reality for a very particular point in time of Vietnamese history, when chữ quốc ngữ (the current Vietnamese script based on Latin characters) had become the standard of education. Many aspects of French culture and language had also started to infiltrate the collective consciousness of Vietnamese society. Despite the push to revolutionise the Vietnamese educational (and therefore, ideological) system completely by imposing French and chữ quốc ngữ on the public, it is quite clear, through the preservation of Sino-Vietnamese words, expressions, and idioms that traditional, pre-French Vietnamese values are still very much imbedded in people's way of life. Vũ Trọng Phụng quotes Beaudelaire just as much as he quotes Nguyễn Du; similarly, in the text there exists both a 'tú bà' (a reference to a character created by *Truyện Kiều's* author, Nguyễn Du—which has now been incorporated into the common Vietnamese lexis—the madam of the brothel who sold

Kiều) and a 'ma-cô' (from the French *maquereau*). In our translation of this text, we seek to preserve the layers of cultural influences that are reflected in Vũ Trọng Phụng's choice of language as much as possible. This means that we sometimes chose to leave the original 'French' in its Vietnamese spelling (often to signify people's inaccurate pronunciation), although there might be an English equivalent.

Since English is limited in comparison to Vietnamese when it comes to the variety of personal pronouns, many aspects of interpersonal relationships which were once expressed simply through designated pronouns now require much more effort to bring across in English. For example, 'cậu' and 'mợ', which mean husband and wife, as well as the patriarch and matriarch of a family unit, is also the way a couple would address one another. In the same way, illeism, a common habit in everyday Vietnamese speech (referring to oneself and your conversing partner by names instead of pronouns), was limited in the English translation, as the switch in first and third-person pronouns can come across as jarring at times. We did not shy away from incorporating footnotes in this text when things deserved some degree of explanation, as we welcome any curious readers who want to learn more about the cultural references mentioned in the text and beyond. However, there are certainly many things that translate better in their untranslated forms.

An example of this matter is the translation of the very

important word/concept that appears in both Vũ Trọng Phụng's (instead of a) preface, and his combative letter against criticism of the novel: 'dâm'. 'Dâm' is translated by Google as 'adultery', probably based on one of the official definitions of the word in Vietnamese as the excessive or illegitimate desire for sex. The word does, in general, have a negative connotation. In Confucius' teachings, he says: 'vạn ác dâm vi thủ', or 'ten thousand evil deeds, adultery stands on top'. This is probably fuelled by the same attitude polite Western society holds towards sex, in that it is a shameful matter. In this sense, would 'lust' not be a better translation, considering the Western reference to the seven deadly sins? Yes, lust is a perfectly acceptable translation, for 'dâm' here very much does mean the desire for sex.

However, with the versatile nature of the Vietnamese language, 'dâm' can also take on a myriad of different connotations by constructing compound words. 'Khiêu dâm' becomes 'pornographic', 'mại dâm' becomes 'prostitution', and 'dâm tặc' is a 'sex offender'. Moreover, when a couple makes love, 'dâm' is also a (often desirable) state of being, an attitude that would hopefully lead to behaviour that is even more 'dâm' ('lewd', in this context). All of this is to highlight the difficulty of trying to find a single English equivalent to such a multi-faceted word/concept.

Yet we have to try, since Vũ Trọng Phụng intentionally repeated this single word throughout his text. To ignore his emphasis and change the translation depending on the context of each sentence would be profound negligence on my part. I try to remain consistent, at least through each of the two texts. In his (instead of a) preface, where the author is defending his views and arguing for a more positive attitude and understanding of 'dâm', I chose to translate it as 'sex'. The neutrality of 'sex' sits right for me here, as the word has both the flexibility and uprightness to be discussed colloquially as well as clinically, which is what Vũ Trọng Phụng does in the original. Towards the end of the (instead of a) preface, 'dâm' starts to become almost empowering, hence I steered clear from any other more negative word choices to embrace Vũ Trọng Phụng's sex-positive attitude.

In the same vein, I wanted to convey the degrading attitude that the critic, Thái Phỉ, adopts in his criticism of Vũ Trọng Phung's novel as 'dâm' in the response text. Here, 'dâm' harbours both Mr. Thái Phỉ's disparaging sentiment and Vũ Trọng Phụng's satirical mockery towards the criticism. I wanted to choose a word that was less neutral, less clinical, more colloquial and more degrading, hence I settled on 'lewd' as the translation of 'dâm' throughout this text. Although this seems like I am going back on my word—about how I should not neglect the author's faithfulness to this single word—but considering the different contexts, replacing one with the other takes away the strength of each translation. Furthermore, 'dâm' in the second text was Mr. Thái Phỉ's word choice, and Vũ

Trọng Phụng only responded in kind; I thus stand by my interpretation that there is a clear difference in each of these men's tone and attitude when they used this word.

Since there is no such thing as a perfectly accurate translation, I am acutely aware of many intricate nuances that were potentially lost during the movement from one language to another. I sincerely welcome our dear readers to express your thoughts. I hope you enjoy the musicality of our tonal language, and try to pronounce the accents without fear. Thank you for reading this wonderful book, and my sincerest gratitude towards Đinh Ngọc Mai for translating this extremely difficult novel.

Sincerely,

Kim from Major Books

Glossary

a dancer girl: a term, gái nhảy in Vietnamese, one of the ways to refer to women doing sex work during French colonial Vietnam. It comes from the French way of referring to sex workers, *cavalière*, literally meaning a dancing girl. There are also potential references to paid dance partner on a dance-by-dance basis in ballroom dancing, popular in America circa 1920s and 30s. The profession was coined as 'taxi dancer'.

Annamite: A demonym for people from Annam. Annam is an old colonial term referring to the French protectorate of Vietnam. It was used in the West as a way to refer to Vietnam as a whole.

cavalier girls: see 'dancer girl'

Chef de Province: Ông Đốc Phủ, the title 'Đốc Phủ Sứ' was the highest rank for Vietnamese officials in the provincial administrative system under French colonial rule in Cochinchina, equivalent to the position of 'Tổng Đốc' (Governor) in Tonkin.

đánh đáo: A Vietnamese traditional game revolving around chucking coins.

đích-tê: Vietnamese pronunciation of the French word 'dictée', a dictation lesson where children practice writing by copying down texts read out loud by teachers in a class

Double Évent, Triple Évent: types of betting in horse-racing.

Elysium: Translated from the Vietnamese expression 'Bồng Lai tiên cảnh', comparable to the Western notion of Elysian field or Shangri-La.

Emperor Gia Long: born Nguyễn Ánh, was the founding

emperor of the Nguyễn dynasty, the last dynasty of Vietnam. His dynasty would rule the unified territories that constitute modern-day Vietnam until 1945.

essayer quelques pas: roughly translates from French as 'try a few steps'

General Cao Biền: was a Chinese military general, poet, and politician of the Tang dynasty.

Hạng Vũ: The Vietnamese transliteration of Xiang Yu, who was enthroned as the 'Hegemon-King of Western Chu'. He engaged Liu Bang, the founding emperor of the Han dynasty, in a long struggle for power, known as the Chu–Han Contention, which concluded with his eventual defeat.

Hmong and Kinh: Two different ethnic groups in Vietnam. The Kinh are the majority, whereas the Hmong mainly reside in the mountains.

Houbigant-perfumed hair: Houbigant (*House of*

Houbigant) is a famous French perfume manufacturer.

jeu des petits chevaux: Roughly translated as 'game of small horses', a French cross and circle game (not unlike ludo)

Kinh hat: Kinh referring to the ethnic majority group in Vietnam, it essentially refers to the hat style that was in vogue amongst upper- and middle-class Vietnamese families of the time.

l'enseignement secondaire: A two-year higher primary school

ma-cô: Vietnamese pronunciation of the French word for pimp (maquereau)

Mán Xá: In Vũ Trọng Phụng's works, Mán Xá is often used as a symbolic or fictional place representing rural or traditional Vietnamese society. The name carries connotations tied to themes of social critique.

Mossant hat: The French brand Mossant was amongst the top hat producers of the time, that sold the fedora hats in fashion amongst well-off men at the time. This western-style hat would be worn by Vietnamese men to show class capital.

New Woman movement: From the Vietnamese 'phong trào gái mới'. In the early 1930s, the 'modern women' movement spread widely across Hanoi. A depiction of a modern Hanoi woman, published in *Phụ nữ Thời đàm* on October 29, 1933, described her as: 'Dressed and adorned in the new style— white trousers, colorful tops, high heels, white teeth, side-parted hair, speaking French with men, occasionally writing articles for newspapers, and having "female writer" on her business card.' However, the article emphasized that 'a modern woman must have new knowledge, new thinking, and, ideally, a new way of living to truly embody modernity.' As attitudes toward women changed, the paper *Phụ nữ Thời đàm*—founded in 1930 and initially conservative— opposed the 'modern' trends. However, after Phan Khôi

became editor-in-chief, the paper shifted to support modern women and even promoted activities like dancing. Despite this, a portion of the population remained opposed, which seems to mirrors Vũ Trọng Phụng's own sentiments

no touching rule between men and women- nam nữ bất tương thân: A Confucian saying from China that deems sacrilegious any physical contact or touch between the opposite sexes.

one wife one husband rule: From the phrase: 'tòng nhất nhi chung', the Vietnamese belief that a woman could only marry once

Pari Mutuel: A betting system where spectators at horse races place wagers against each other, with the racetrack management acting as an intermediary. A portion of the winnings is deducted to support charitable activities.

Paris Plaisirs, Eros, and Sex Appeal: Erotic magazines of the time

primaire élémentaire:
Equivalent to today's primary
school—the first level of
education of three years, taught
in Vietnamese

prix d'honneur: A prize
that awards the best student
in class, in colonial-era
Vietnamese education.

sex appeal: In the original,
this is a direct reference to the
American expression 'sex-
appeal' circulating at the time.

*the Longchamp 2200-metre
championship*: Longchamp in
Paris is home to a famous horse
racing track. At other horse
racing venues, the biggest
prize is often referred to as the
Longchamp Prize.

*three subordinations and four
virtues*: a translation of '*Tam
tòng, tứ đức*', or '三从四德' in
Chinese, refers to the Confucian
set of social codes for women,
which involved expectations of
the woman's place in society,
how she should act etc. Due
to Chinese colonisation and
influence on Vietnam, these
virtues helped shape the gender
dynamics in Vietnam.

Western secret agent: An agent
of the French colonial police
bureau in Vietnam, '*Sûreté
général indochinoise*', a vital part
of the colonial administration
that operated from 1917 till
1945, tasked to help maintain
French colonial dominance.

Coming soon from Major Books

The Tale of Kiều

A new translation in verse of a national classic that has enchanted readers across generations and shaped the cultural landscape of Vietnam.—epic poem by Nguyễn Du, translated by Nguyễn Bình, first publication estimated circa 1821 (still debated)

Parallel

Widely considered as the best Vietnamese gay fiction. Unapologetic and daring, this book deserves to be on the same shelf with the sexiest works by some of the best living gay writers.—novel by Vũ Đình Giang, translated by Khải Q. Nguyễn, first published in 2007